T0354560

The Bounty Hunters

Joey Hoffman

Order this book online at www.trafford.com
or email orders@trafford.com

Most Trafford titles are also available at major online book retailers.

Printed in the United States of America.

ISBN: 978-1-4669-7386-2 (sc)
ISBN: 978-1-4669-7388-6 (hc)
ISBN: 978-1-4669-7387-9 (e)

Library of Congress Control Number: 2012924022

Trafford rev. 01/10/2013

www.trafford.com

North America & international
toll-free: 1 888 232 4444 (USA & Canada)
phone: 250 383 6864 ♦ fax: 812 355 4082

CONTENTS

CHAPTER ONE

Their First Bounty

It was a race against time for Matt Jax and William Hoffman to locate and apprehend the lawless and dangerous criminal, Conrad Larson.

Travis, who was barely nineteen and fresh out of the police academy, was busy punching the keys on the computer, bringing Conrad's file to view. "He's in Coeur d'Alene, over on Lakeside Avenue."

"Let's go get him," Matt, half owner of his new company, THE UNDERDOGS, ordered to his partner William and their young apprentice, Travis. "We have until midnight to collect on his bounty."

Travis printed out some copies of Conrad's photo, then joined his elders in gearing up. He wore his baggy blue jeans and white sneakers with a large container of chemical spray strapped onto his thigh. He exhibited his badge and chain about his neck while Matt and William wore their medal stars upon their belts. They carried bulletproof vests, handcuffs, and walkie-talkies to the SUV, then drove to the city.

As they entered Coeur d'Alene, the sky brought forth showers. They exited the freeway and headed west on Sherman Avenue, the main artery to downtown.

"I wish we had Nick to help us on this one," Travis remarked, "We need more man power."

"Aaww, what's the matter?" William jested from the front passenger seat as he turned his head toward Travis and winked. "Can't you handle Conrad?"

Travis smirked.

"I kind of think," Matt replied, "that Nick's lost interest in bounty hunting, he'd rather roof. And Nathan's too young. Dominique won't let him get involved until he's eighteen." He turned the vehicle onto Twenty-First Street, then veered left on Lakeside.

Travis was eager as he sat in the rear seat holding onto the door handle. His gut churned while they drove by each house, eyeing the address numbers. He had his training and watched many accounts of captures on television, but to chase and apprehend criminals in real life seemed more frightening, and he knew Matt felt the same way.

Matt drove to the next block, turned his vehicle around, and parked alongside the curb near the corner. He and William spied Conrad's property through their binoculars.

"I see him," William stated. "He's walking around his yard and it look's like he's picking up some toys." He set his optical device down and looked at Matt. "Travis and I will slink up the alleyway and take him by surprise."

"Make double sure it's him before apprehending," Matt advised as they exited the vehicle. "We don't need any unforeseen trouble such as a lawsuit."

"Sure."

While Travis and William went around the block to creep through the narrow passageway, Matt walked the sidewalk near the fugitive's house to keep watch on the front area.

Thunder rumbled throughout the gray sky with promise of heavy rain.

Matt halted before coming upon his yard and withdrew behind a large maple tree. He observed Conrad looking up at the clouds, then watched him step to his truck. Thinking he was going to leave, he brought his walkie-talkie to his mouth, but then stopped. After opening the driver's door, Conrad rolled up the window.

Matt radioed his position to his comrades.

"Ten-four," William replied, "We're coming up on the back yard now." They entered through an open gateway and stepped across the wet grass to the rim of the garage. William peeked around the edge and saw their culprit keying the garage door. He caught sight of the tattoo on his cheek, then stepped out into view holding a taser gun. "You stop right there where you stand Conrad!" he ordered.

Conrad gyrated and took off running.

Travis sprinted after him with William in tow.

"He's coming your way," William transmitted to Matt over his radio.

Conrad ran across the driveway toward the side of his house. As he rounded the corner, he tripped on his footing, tumbling over a metal garbage can.

Just as Conrad uprooted himself to his feet, Travis leaped onto his back, flattening his bounty into a small mud puddle. William and Matt were right there, handcuffing their wet prisoner.

"Stand him up," Matt roared as he viewed Conrad's appearance. "Why didn't you go to court?"

"I guess I got the dates wrong," he answered rudely.

Travis began to pat him down. "Do you have anything sharp or illegal in your pockets?"

He was silent for a moment, then spoke, "Yea, I have a pipe in my front pocket."

Travis pulled the metal device from the pouch along with a small bud wrapped in plastic wrap. "Why you smoking this shit?" he scolded, "You already have drug charges against you."

Conrad shrugged his shoulders. "I like my weed."

Matt understood how he felt as he listened in.

Travis handed the illegals to his step dad to destroy. "You're lucky we don't turn this in, but rather toss it out." He led the bounty across the yard to the SUV where he seat belted him in. Matt and William hopped into the front seats and headed to the jail.

Matt had sympathy for their prisoner who asked to smoke one last cigarette before being booked, so he steered and parked in a vacant lot where he re-handcuffed Conrad in the frontal region and enjoyed a tobacco stick himself.

Ian, a scared boy of ten, came rushing into the house with fear written upon his face. He locked the front door, then hastened across the living room floor and through the kitchen where he also locked the back door.

Dominique was in awe as she watched her son crawl underneath the table. "What's the matter?" She stepped to and knelt beside the wooden structure.

He paused a moment while he took a few breaths. "Damian has a knife."

"Are you hurt?"

"No, but he almost stabbed me."

"Why?" She exhibited concern as she yielded to serious thought. "Why did he have a knife?"

"I don't know."

"Yes you do know."

"I told him he couldn't jump on our trampoline."

She thought for a moment. "Was he going to use that knife to cut on the trampoline too?"

He shrugged his shoulders.

Dominique arose to her feet and whirled herself around. She walked to and unlocked the back door, then exited the house.

Matt was stopped at a red light when Conrad, full of stealth, clicked his seat belt and quickly lifted the door handle.

"Don't you do it!" Travis warned as he reached his arms out and tried to seize the perpetrator, but he was already out the door and running. Before he could remove his own seat belt, Matt stepped on the gas pedal. "Stop the car!" he yelled, then jumped onto the street as the vehicle slowed.

"What the hell?" Matt cast his vision to the empty rear seat, then saw Travis giving chase to Conrad who had already cleared a lot and was rounding the corner of a building. He pressed the accelerator and sped to the next block where he backtracked on the side streets toward the area of pursuit.

Travis radioed to Matt and William, wanting their assistance. "Where are you guys? He's getting far ahead of me." He panted for air between messages. "He's on Anton Street, heading toward the Town Square, over."

"We're on Fifth Street. There's traffic slowing us down, over."

William turned to Matt. "Drop me off up here at the corner, I'll hopefully catch him coming this way."

Matt let him out of the Explorer at the stop sign and continued on to the plaza. He transmitted to Travis, their positions.

Travis was in the alley behind the stores. Conrad had vanished from his sight. He slowed his running, quickly searching inside and around the dumpsters.

William was guarding the southeast end of the parking lot while Matt scouted the west end from his SUV. William rounded the corner of a large retail store and bumped into Travis.

"That guy can run!" Travis remarked while his eyes roamed the area. "I wonder if he'll head back to his house?"

"Probably not right away," he replied, then radioed to Matt. "Travis and I are over here on the northeast corner and we lost him."

"There he is!" Travis blurted as he pointed, then sent word to Matt to get the vehicle to them now.

William spun around and saw that the rookie was pointing at a moving pickup truck.

"He's in the back of that truck!"

William, with his blazing blue eyes, also observed Conrad's head bobbing from the rim of the bed as though he was peeking to see if he was being followed.

Matt sped to his buddies. They jumped into the Explorer and Matt raced off through the parking lot and out onto Appleway Avenue. They traveled east, following their culprit from afar. Matt drove about a mile, then turned south on Fifteenth Street.

"He's heading toward I-90. We need to get him before he gets on the freeway."

"Pull up beside the truck," William proposed from the passenger's seat. "I have an idea."

With no traffic coming from the opposite direction, Matt yielded to his partner's dangerous request in spite of his fear.

William drew his pistol from his shoulder holster, rolled down his window, and as they came upon the driver of the pickup truck, he aimed the weapon at him.

The old fellow displayed fright when he saw William's badge and pistol so he slowed and maneuvered his truck to the side of the road.

With a downpour now in session, Travis opened his door and stepped on the wet sideboard. Before both vehicles could stop, the slim bounty hunter sprang up onto the ledge of the truck and lunged for

Conrad who was preparing to jump to the ground from the other end of the bed.

Conrad struggled until he saw William aiming his pistol at him.

Matt climbed into the bed of the truck and together, he and Travis re-handcuffed their escapee to his backside, stood him up, and escorted him back to their SUV.

The driver of the truck apologized, "I didn't know he was back there."

Matt waved the elderly man off, then returned to his vehicle.

Ian advanced from underneath the table and followed his mother to the back yard where she checked the trampoline, then headed toward the gate that led to the driveway.

Dominique told Ian to wait by the open gate while she talked to Damian's parents.

Some two minutes later, she returned to Ian.

"What happened?" he asked.

"They caught him with the knife; he's in trouble, but if he does it again, I'M calling the cops."

"Good."

She looked down at him. "If he comes over to our yard, I want you to come tell me. I want to keep an eye on him." She felt raindrops falling from the sky as they entered the house.

Dominique set the dining room table and checked on dinner. She took a glance at the clock and wondered if her family would be late. She knew her husband would call when and if he could.

Nathan, Dominique's third born, entered through the rear door. "I'm home Mom!" He took a chair from the kitchen table and plopped down on it.

As she leaned her backside against the counter, she eyed his grubby jeans and dusty boots.

"I'm tired," His brown hair was marked by confusion and his face bore uncombed sideburns. There was dirt in the corner of his eyes.

"How'd you get so dirty playing video games?"

"Sandy's mom came home. She was being a bitch so we left."

"Where did you go?"

"We hiked up to the Glen."

She knew the Glen was their fort located somewhere on the mountainside of Kellogg or Wardner. "Did his mom know where you were?"

"No."

"You need to tell someone where you're going to be."

"I'll be okay Mom, I'm almost a man."

"Things can still happen," she cautioned.

Matt and Travis advanced through the rear door of the house. Matt ran a comb through his thick black hair as he stepped to Dominique. "What a day we had," he remarked, "I'll tell you about it later." He kissed her with a quick peck on the cheek.

"That was a sister kiss, I want a wife kiss."

"You'll get what you get," he jested.

"Brat!"

While Travis went to the shower, Matt withdrew to his bedroom. He removed from his pocket, Conrad's pipe and bud. He tossed the metal vessel into the garbage after inspecting it, then loaded some of the bud into his own pipe. "Thank you Conrad!" he said.

CHAPTER TWO

Family Matters

It was the second half of the game. The hundred and eighty-five pound teenager who was defending his team's goalkeeper, ran toward the penalty area where an opposing player was setting himself up to receive the ball.

The soccer ball was sent in midair to Nathan's opponent who, as he lifted a leg to kick the ball, fell to his backside. Nathan leaped into the air and with his shoulder, he blocked the play from his rival's perfect bicycle kick. The crowd cheered.

Nathan scanned for a teammate while he nudged the ball ahead a yard. He thrust the round object to the center line where a midfielder took over and kicked it to a forward. The forward obtained control, dribbled, and baffled a challenger with his footwork before kicking and scoring a goal. The game was won by Nathan's team, three to one.

As Nathan walked with his mom and younger brother to their car, he noticed within a group of people, a girl he recognized from school, waving at him. He politely returned the greeting, then took a drink from his water bottle.

Ian witnessed the salutation and told his mom. "Nathan has a girlfriend."

"No I don't. I don't even know her," he denied with a smile.

Matt spent the morning at the office helping William arrange the desks and furniture into their places. They had the lease, the licenses framed and nailed onto the freshly painted wall, and their new sign hung above the exterior door. The Underdogs were officially in business.

The technician was busy installing the cables and connecting the wires to the computers.

After William left to run a few errands, Matt distributed pens to both desks. He then removed two staplers and two paper receptacles from a shopping bag and placed each into their spots. He opened the top drawer of his partner's desk and saw a pornographic magazine. He smiled as he took hold of it, then he sat onto William's chair and thumbed through it. "Mmm." He turned a few pages more. "Ohh . . . I'll take her." The telephone rang, startling him. He answered it.

"Are you almost done?"

"Yea, I'm just arranging the stuff onto the desks," he told his wife. "I'll be home in about a half an hour."

"Good," she replied. "We're firing up the barbecue soon."

The day was sporting a blue sky and sunshine. Dominique and her three youngest sons were enjoying their Saturday afternoon amidst the outdoors. She had her long blonde hair clipped up out of her face while she weeded her flower garden.

Travis was washing his truck in the rear driveway and Nathan was scrubbing the metal rack from the grill with a steel wool soap pad, one of his mom's last minute requests. Ian was jumping merrily upon the trampoline.

After Dominique uprooted the last weed, she twisted two yellow pansies by their stems until they broke loose. She arose to her feet and relished the scent of the flowers through her pointy nose. She carried the waste bucket to the larger garbage can in the alley and dumped the unwanted plants. She lifted her head and saw a silver pickup truck approaching quite fast, then it came to a sudden stop. She smiled at the driver.

"Hi Mom!" Nick greeted as he stepped out of his vehicle.

"I thought you had to work today?"

"I did this morning. We finished the shingling by noon so we got the hell out of there."

William soon returned to the office with a twelve pack of beer. "This calls for a celebration." He handed one to Matt, then opened one for himself.

"You bet it does. I've always wanted to run my own business and now I do." He rested himself into his chair and propped his feet onto the edge of his desk. "I also have a great partner to share it with."

"Please don't make me cry!" he joked.

From across the room, Matt held his can up in the air as though he was toasting, then drank.

"Cheers," William replied, then took a drink. "I usually don't drink, only on special occasions."

"Well I think this is a special occasion."

"Cheers!"

After a while, Matt asked his partner to help him look up something on the computer since he really didn't know the device too well.

"What do you need?"

"I need to find my niece."

He exposed a confused, but curious look. "Don't you know where she lives or can't you just call her parents?" He thought, then continued. "Which would be your brother or sister?"

"No. Rainy is my twin sister's girl. My sister died four years ago just as I found out she was my sister."

"Sorry about your loss there buddy."

"Rainy's turning eighteen in a few days so now I can legally look her up."

"Okay." He took hold of a pen and a piece of paper. "What's her full name?"

"Rainy June Waubay."

"Is that her mom or dad's last name?"

"My sister's name was Nisa Waubay. I don't think she ever married." He paused. "Too long of a story, but I was given up for adoption and our mom Tilly kept Nisa. I just thought I'd throw that in there."

"You poor thing," he joked, but was still serious. "When is Rainy's birthday?"

"June tenth. She was born on a rainy June day."

William wrote the date down. "Do you know her social security number?" He glanced at him.

Matt shook his head no.

"Anything else that would help?"

"Nisa had an Aunt Penny. I guess she would have been mine too. She use to live in Phoenix, but after Nisa died, she moved away."

"Is her last name Waubay?"

"I don't know."

"We'll start with Rainy." He turned his computer on and typed the appropriate keys to get to the internet, then into the telephone directory data base.

Matt stepped just outside the open doorway to smoke a cigarette.

"I have several R Waubay's,"William called out from across the room. "It'll take you all day, maybe two to call every number."

"Can you narrow it down or look somewhere else?"

"Maybe and yes."

Matt butted his cigarette and returned to his desk chair where he cracked open another beer. He quietly waited while William searched through the driver's license data base.

"I came up with one Rainy J. Waubay who has the same birthdate. She lives on Fourteenth Street in Eloy, Arizona." He whirled in his swivel chair and cast his vision onto his partner. "You do have to remember, people move so often, she might not be there anymore."

Matt rubbed his bristly chin in heavy thought on what to do. "Is there any way of finding out what phone number matches that address?"

"Dial 411." He printed out the lists from both information sources and handed them to his associate.

Matt looked them over. "You're right, there are a lot."

William turned off his computer and announced he was going home. "I'll leave you the rest of the beer. Two is plenty for me."

Matt dialed 411, but the operator told him there was no telephone number for that person. He then highlighted with his yellow marker, all the R. Waubays from Arizona. As he drank on another beer, he took the receiver from the telephone and dialed his first number.

"Hello?"

"Hi, I'm looking for Rainy," he somewhat slurred his request.

"You have the wrong number."

"Who does the R represent, may I ask?"

"Ronny."

Matt placed the handset on to the base, then crossed out and wrote Ronny beside the number. His second call revealed a Ruben, the third, no one answered, and the fourth call announced that the line had been disconnected. "This is going to be a lot of work," he told himself as he rested his elbows onto the desk and put his hands over his face.

The sun was kissing the mountaintops good night when Dominique set Matt's leftovers in the refrigerator and cleaned up after her family's barbecue dinner. Ian was ordered into the bathtub and Travis left to go visit a friend. Nathan remained outdoors with Nick.

"You're ten years old Ian, you're old enough to wash your own hair and feet," Dominique scolded her son from the bathroom doorway after he earnestly pressed for help.

Nick slipped a cd into his new truck stereo and cranked it briefly to boast of its power to his younger brother.

"Awesome," Nathan remarked after Nick turned it down. "How much did that cost you?"

Before he could answer, he and Nathan heard Matt yelling as he approached from across the yard. "Turn that crap off! You can hear it clear in the front yard."

With confusion written upon his face, Nick looked at Nathan, then whirled himself around and responded. "If you go into the house, you won't even hear it."

Steam arose from Matt's countenance. "No kid is going to tell ME to go into MY own house!" he roared.

Nathan stepped back and stood by the anterior of the truck where he watched and listened intently.

"It was only a suggestion." Nick began to raise his voice in defense. "Besides, I'm not a kid. I'm twenty-one years old."

"Yea, you are a man." He stepped up to him. "Does that mean you're now a Billy Bad Ass?"

"Get out of my face," Nick warned as he went backwards a few feet. He could smell the rank alcohol coming from his mouth.

"YOU go home and go in YOUR house!" he slurred to him.

What an idiot, Nick thought. "What's your problem?"

"I don't have a problem." He jabbed his finger into his stepson's chest. "And I'll say it again . . ."

"Don't touch me!" Nick spoke bravely, interrupting him.

Nathan's eyes widened. He was becoming dismayed as he witnessed the man who promised to cherish his new family cause trouble.

"You've got all the balls in the world, don't you?" Matt continued his drunken display as he stood unsteadily.

"Get out of my face or I'm going to hit you." He recalled from watching his first step dad Andrew fight, how to draw a fist with his thumb outside of his fingers then put force into the punch.

"No, I won't get out of your face. You're nothing but a spoiled brat and you're not going to tell me what to do. I tell you what to do."

"No—you don't tell me what to do." Nick's tolerance was growing penny thin as he again stepped back, hoping Matt would leave. He didn't want to resort to violence for his mom's sake.

"I told you to go home." Matt followed him to the other side of his vehicle. "Get into your truck!"

Nick had enough. He clinched his fist and after he rotated himself about, he stepped forward and with great might, he swung a closed hand, making contact on Matt's yapping jaw.

As Matt soared backwards to the ground, his top dentures came out of his mouth and flew through the air. He was out cold.

"Oh shit!" Nathan exclaimed as he joined his brother who was examining his knuckles.

They stared at Matt. Through the dusk, they could see the blood that was trickling from the corner of his mouth, then they noticed his broken teeth that lay just ten feet or so away upon the gravel.

Matt began to move.

"I'm leaving." Nick stepped to and climbed into his truck.

"I'm coming with you." Nathan hurried to the passenger side of the truck and as Nick drove away, Matt staggered to his feet and headed toward the house.

"We need to tell mom." Nick lit a cigarette and puffed.

"Just drive around for a few minutes before you take me back home," he suggested, "And drop me off at the front door."

CHAPTER THREE

Matt's Quest

Dominique awoke alone the next morning. As she sat up, she noticed Matt's side of the bed was untouched and nearly crease free. She lit a cigarette and arose to her feet. After using the toilet, she went to the living room to see if perhaps Matt was sleeping on the couch. The sofa was bare. She then stepped to the bay window and looked out; Matt's truck was absent from its spot. Her heart ached. She wondered where her husband had spent the night after his ridiculous display of drunkenness.

Dominique returned to her bedroom, to her bathroom, and showered. She then woke Ian and Nathan for church.

Matt didn't show up at the Lord's house for service and when noon arrived, she shook hands with the pastor and made a quick exit. With her two sons, she drove by a few local motels spying for her husband's truck. She cruised by THE UNDERDOG'S office, then took a quick trip out to her mother-in-law's house. After no sign of Matt's truck, she went home; maybe he was there by now.

Inside her house, she advanced to her vacant bedroom and when she set her Bible and car keys onto her dresser, she saw Matt's wedding ring and bank card placed on his side of the bureau. Her heart dropped. She took a side step, snatched up the golden band, and as she held it within her fingers, a tear dripped from her eye. Under the debit card was a small piece of paper that manifested two words. "I quit!" Her mouth went dry as she read it. Was her marriage really over? She wondered.

"I want these trees trimmed and this yard cleaned up before I get home. You have a month," Luke Senior mandated to his twin sons Luke Junior and Reddy who stood on the back porch of their house and visually eyed the property. "Don't just pile and leave the dead branches. Burn them. Also, cut the overgrowth, plant the seeds and water them, and paint the fence." He pointed as he spoke. "Basically, I want you two to make this yard look as though it could be the Garden of Eden."

"It'll get done Pa," Luke Junior replied as he lit himself a cigarette.

"I also want," Luke Senior whispered, "you to keep a close eye on Critter. No boys! She's only fifteen and still innocent. Your mother would roll over in her grave if anything happened to her baby girl."

"She's in good hands."

Luke Senior soon kissed his daughter good bye, took hold of and carried his suitcase out to his truck, then left for his job in Alaska.

The blond twins returned to the inside of the house and sat on the couch. After inserting a game into the video system, Reddy picked up his controller and pressed play. Luke Junior joined him as they battled the aliens together.

Critter entered into the living room. "You two better get on that back yard. You'll be lucky to get that whole acre done by the time Pa gets home."

They ignored her.

"Did you hear me?" she asked.

"Yea we heard you," one answered.

"We need to hire us a worker," the other brother suggested while their sister remained in the threshold and listened.

"With what money? Pa didn't leave us any for that."

Reddy thought. "We need us a slave then," he remarked as he displayed extreme effort in pushing the controller buttons. "We'll never beat these aliens if we have to work."

Matt was now sober and had been driving for two days when he came into Southern Arizona. He arrived on the outskirts of Phoenix where he rented himself a motel room.

Inside his room, he sat on the edge of the bed and as he smoked a cigarette, he eyed the telephone. He thought about calling Dominique, then decided not to. He lifted and opened the large telephone book and looked under the w's. All the R Waubay's listed, he had already called from Idaho. He then handled a smaller phone book and turned to the w's. After seeing the same R Waubay's, he moved his finger up to a P Waubay. "Could that be Aunt Penny?" He took hold of the receiver and dialed nine, then the number. He let it ring five times before hanging up. He noted the Eloy address as he ripped the page from the book, then stuffed the folded leaf into his pocket.

Matt arose to his feet and stepped to the window where he pulled the curtain aside and peeked out. He cast his vision here and there, eyeing the nearby businesses. His eyes widened when he saw a strip club down the street.

Dominique set the receiver from the phone down on the base and remained sitting at her desk. She used her arm to prop her head and rest her chin on her palm as she gazed out the window.

Travis came walking by his mom's office door and looked in. "Was that Matt on the phone?"

"No, that was William."

"Has he seen Matt?"

"All he said about Matt was that he will be back in a few days. He also wanted you to call him tomorrow morning."

The next morning after Matt awoke, he thought about last night; the beautiful blonde stripper, how he paid her to take a dollar bill off his face, but not with her hands or mouth. As he laid in bed and sexually pleased himself, he started to feel guilty—his heart still yearned for Dominique.

Soon he was showered and ready for a day of investigating. He dialed the Eloy telephone number once again for P Waubay; still no one answered. He left in his truck.

After an hour of driving south toward the little town of Eloy, he exited from the interstate. He soon turned from Highway 84, drove a few blocks before turning east, then north to Fourteenth Street where he drove slow on the residential street, reading the house numbers. When he came upon the correct address, he parked alongside the curb and stepped out. He quickly looked about the area as he advanced to the door of the casa.

He knocked and no one came to open the door so he stepped to the nearby window and peeked in; all was dim inside. As he walked to his truck, he eyed the neighbor's house, contemplating whether to ask them for information or not, then reminded himself he was a bounty hunter. "Of course I'll go ask."

A plump woman with auburn hair opened the entry way door. "Yes?"

"Hi. I'm looking for the person who lives next door there." He pointed. "Could you tell me if you know them or know when they'll be home?"

"And who are you?"

In spite of her rudeness, he answered. "My name's Matt Jax. I'm searching for Rainy Waubay."

"I thought I recognized you," the woman replied with a straight face.

Matt produced a look of muddle. Why was Aunt Penny at THIS house? "Same here, but I thought you maybe lived next door."

"I use to. I bought this house and . . ." She paused. "Come on in Mathew." She widened the entrance.

He entered with much observation.

"Do you even know what Rainy looks like?" she asked him.

He thought that was an odd first question. "No. I do know she's turned eighteen and I want to tell her who I am."

"We should probably tell her together." She led him into the living room to the sofa. "Rainy does live next door with her beau, Adam Bow."

He smiled at the rhyme. "Do you know when she'll get home?"

She glanced at the clock as she reached for a picture on her shelf. "They left about seven-thirty this morning so I'm guessing soon. She's driving Adam around, looking for work."

"Oh yea?" He looked down at the photo of his niece as he held it in his hands. "She's beautiful. She looks like Nisa."

"She looks like you too. You and your sister had, have the same eyebrows."

There was a moment of silence. "What kind of work is Adam looking for?"

"He was checking into a few security guard jobs."

"You two should get working on the yard," Critter urged, "Pa's been gone three days now and you've done nothing."

"It'll happen, don't worry," Luke replied.

Some half hour later and Reddy turned off the television and carried an armful of dirty dishes and food wrappers from the coffee table to the kitchen.

Luke stretched after he arose from the couch, then headed toward and through the exterior door of the house to the back porch where he joined Reddy.

Reddy had a paintbrush in one hand and a gallon of dark blue paint in the other.

"What are you doing?" Luke who wore an odd look upon his face, called out to his brother.

Reddy glanced at his twin as he approached and stood beside the fence. "I'm going to paint."

"Not yet. We have to trim and burn the branches first, move rocks, landscape and rototill. Painting is last," he tried to explain sensibly.

"That's all hard work. I just wanted to do something easy right now."

"You're just wasting time and money," Luke scolded.

"No I'm not. I'll just paint the top boards."

"That's stupid!"

"You're just mad cuz I beat you at Alienoids."

"Now that's irrelevant."

"There you go with your big fancy words," Reddy spoke with a saucy tongue.

"It means that the video game has nothing to do with this conversation."

"I don't care!"

"Well I do." Luke stepped forward, grabbed and lifted the can of paint by the thin arched handle.

Reddy lunged and when he seized the open can, it spilled over onto Luke's pant leg and shoe.

"Smooth move Retard!"

In a fit of anger, Reddy flung the can of paint about the yard, letting the colored liquid spatter upon the nearby bushes and the ground, then he tossed the container to the pile of rocks.

Luke held in the rest of his thoughts as he turned away and returned to the porch where he took off his shoes and pants.

Reddy stood idle until Luke went into the house.

Critter stepped outside to the rear porch of their Pinecreek home. "I hid your video games."

"I don't care." Reddy picked up a large rock and carried it to the far side of the yard where he heaved it over the rugged fence.

Matt and Aunt Penny walked next door after Adam and Rainy arrived home. Matt took in a deep breath as he entered into his niece's living room.

"Hi Auntie," Rainy greeted as she stood beside her end table. "Look what I bought." She held up a skirt.

Matt grasped her appearance; her long black hair, green eyes, and her petite figure.

"Rainy, Sweetheart?" Aunt Penny spoke, "I have someone here who wants to meet you and you should meet him too."

Rainy eyed the stranger, glanced at Adam who was sitting on the couch watching and listening, then cast her vision onto her great aunt.

"This is your Uncle Mathew. He's your mom's twin brother."

She cracked a little smile. "Hello."

Matt stepped closer to her. "I'm glad to be finally meeting you. I never knew Nisa all that well, she passed away shortly after I met her."

Rainy looked at her aunt with confusion.

"It's a long story. Let's go talk in your bedroom."

After the two women walked off, Matt sat on the couch, the far side from Adam. "So I hear you're looking for security work?" Matt broke the awkward silence between them.

"Yea, I put in a few aps today."

"What kind of experience do you have?"

"I went to the police academy and dropped out."

"You didn't like it?"

"Na—the commanding officer was a real dick."

"I'm a bounty hunter. Me and my partner William just started our own business."

"Oh yea?" His eyes widened.

"In Idaho. We're actually looking for another guy." He noted Adam's broad shoulders and muscular frame. "You look strong enough to handle a fleeing bail jumper."

"I could probably catch you a few."

Matt rubbed his chin in thought as he looked off, then cast his vision onto Adam and spoke with enthusiasm. "It's something to think about, but you and Rainy could come up to Idaho and take a course on bounty hunting while you train with our company. We'll even pay for the classes."

"I'll have to talk to Rainy about it, but I don't foresee any problems."

"Sounds fair to me."

Travis turned off the engine and exited his vehicle. He advanced to the building, into the small office of The Underdogs, and joined William for a day of work.

"Quest Bail Bonds called. Swade needs us to go pick up a woman who didn't show up for her court hearing."

"Coeur d' Alene?"

"Somewhere in that vicinity, but we're not gearing up for the first stint," William informed. "We have to go in and find us a Judas. There's limited info on this gal according to Swade." He arose from his chair with his handcuffs and badge and led the way to the outside, then locked the office door. They drove to the city.

Inside the bail bonds agency, William obtained a power of attorney and a photo from the bondsman, then stepped to Travis and recommended he outfit himself into a delivery man's uniform. "Swade called our culprit's home phone yesterday and it's been disconnected so you're going fishing," he spoke to the rookie as he searched through a few papers. "Other info. She drives a small car—um . . . a silver Ford Festiva."

They left the business district of Coeur d' Alene and drove a few miles to the apartment complex where Misty lives.

"I don't see her car anywhere," William remarked.

Travis took an envelope from their box of supplies and wrote Misty's name and address on it before stepping out of the parked SUV. William watched through his binoculars while Travis approached her apartment and knocked.

After no one answered, Travis stepped to the window and peeked in; it was vacant. He pulled his cell phone from his pocket and buzzed his partner, letting him know he was en route to the landlord's office.

William exited the company vehicle with Misty's photo and walked toward a small group of youngsters who were investing their energy into a little ball throwing. "Who wants a reward?" He asked them as he waved a few dollar bills around.

The kids stepped to him and examined the photo of Misty. Most replied they didn't know her. One girl recalled seeing the fugitive carry a suitcase to her car, but that was all she knew.

Travis returned from the landlord's with no forwarding address for Misty, however, he obtained her mother's address. "I had to tell him I was a bounty hunter to get that information." He climbed into the SUV.

"Good work," William commended as he turned the key then drove away.

Travis changed out of the delivery shirt and reverted to his t-shirt. He also armed himself in his usual gear including his pistol.

They soon arrived at their next destination. The two agents left their vehicle and approached the entry of the mother's house. Travis knocked, then scanned the nearby window for movement.

A woman eased the door open, keeping the guard chain attached. "What do you want?" she asked.

"We want Misty!" William commanded in his firm deep voice.

"She ain't here."

"Are you sure?" His intimidating tone seemed to of not frighten her.

"And who are you to be demanding?" she snapped.

"Excuse me Ma'am," William softened his voice as he exhibited his badge. "We're bounty hunters. Your daughter didn't show up for court."

The woman sighed. "I'm tired of her drinking and dopin' so I'll tell you that she frequents Chubby's Bar down on Sherman Avenue with her boyfriend. I hope that helps you."

"What's the boyfriend's name?"

"Andy."

"She moved out of her apartment," William disclosed, hoping for more information.

"I didn't know that. She only calls me every couple of weeks or so."

"How do you get a hold of her?"

"I don't."

"If you hear from her, please give us a call." He handed her one of his business cards through the gap, then turned and left the porch, leaving the property.

"You think she's in there?" Travis asked him.

"No."

"Let me guess—we're going to Chubby's?"

"You're catching on real quick."

William and Travis entered the tavern as plain clothed men, sat at the bar and ordered chicken strips n' fries. They cast their eyes about the establishment, but neither of the two women in there were Misty.

The bartender approached them with their lemonades.

"I'm looking for Misty," William asked him as he showed her photo.

"Haven't seen her in a few days," he replied.

The two agents finished eating and left the building. When they neared their SUV, a somewhat intoxicated man came from behind and tapped Travis on the shoulder. He whirled around, prepared to protect himself.

"I can tell you where Misty is," the man slurred, "but it'll cost you."

Travis threw a questionable glance at William, then returned his sights onto the stranger. "Oh yea? How much you want?"

"Fifty dollars!"

"I'll give you twenty-five," he demanded the compromise.

The drunkard held out his hand for the money. "They went to Kennewick."

"Where in Kennewick?"

"I don't know. I didn't catch their whole conversation."

"You better not be lying to us or we'll have to come back and kick your ass," William threatened.

Matt arrived in Kellogg with a gut full of butterflies, unsure of Dominique's reaction to his leaving and returning. He downed a cigarette rather quickly before entering into their large house. He searched and found her sitting at the desk inside her office. As he neared, he saw that her face sported a cold glare. "Dominique, I was an idiot."

"Yes, you were."

"I made a mistake."

She knew what he was wanting. "You think after five days of being gone with no phone calls, you can waltz in here and expect me to take you back?"

"No, I don't expect, I'm just hoping." His words were flavored with pity.

She arose from her chair and stood toward the window, her back against him. "You left your wedding ring on the dresser. What am I suppose to think?"

"I don't know."

"Where's your heart Matt? Is it really here with me?" She turned to peek at his reaction, then looked away.

"Yes, I want to be with you."

She was quiet as she considered his words and her feelings.

"I'll cut down on my drinking," he spoke to sway her.

She figured he meant well for now. "I didn't appreciate what you did to Nick. How dare you try to fight him!"

"Like I said Dominique, I was an idiot!"

CHAPTER FOUR

The Taking Of Nathan

William returned to Coeur d' Alene and learned from Misty' mother, of another daughter. He also obtained her Kennewick address, then early the next morning with Travis and Nick, he drove three hours to the Mid-Columbia city.

"Thanks for helping today Nick. With Matt taking the day off, I need the extra pair of eyes," William remarked.

"No problem. I'll work for you, but not for Matt or with Matt."

"Don't like him much, huh?" He took a sip of coffee from his mug.

"Never did."

The trio arrived just as the sun was spreading its splendor. William traveled Highway 395 to Clearwater Avenue, then backtracked on the smaller roads to Mataline Avenue. After locating the address and pinpointing the correct apartment, he parked the SUV. He used his binoculars to spy the dwelling and saw that the curtains were closed. "Now we sit and wait."

"Let's just storm the place, go in and grab this chick," Nick suggested.

"It's illegal to enter into the home of friends or family members just to look."

"Then I propose that I go knock on the door and pretend to be looking for someone?"

"At five-thirty in the morning?"

Travis turned himself from the passenger seat and threw a grin at his brother who then returned the gesture.

"Patience Nick," William spoke, "We'll get her."

Two hours passed by with no movement from the named apartment and Nick was becoming antsy. "I need a cigarette," he remarked.

"Go walk down the street and smoke one," William told him, "Keep your radio on."

As he ambled down the sidewalk, he gave thought to creeping about the back side of the complex. Why not? It's a good idea he concluded, so he gently tilted his vision toward the rear of the SUV to see that William and Travis were still sitting inside, then he stepped around the corner. He advanced to the posterior end of the building and came upon an open bathroom window. He wanted to catch her showering, then decided to not spy, but rather take a brief look only as he continued on.

After he rounded the far side of the complex, he saw a man exiting from the apartment. "Andy?" he asked himself, then quickly tucked his radio away and hustled toward him. "Excuse me Sir—I'm looking for my girlfriend's black cat. She escaped from our apartment just ten minutes ago."

"Haven't seen any black cat around."

Nick looked away as though he was searching the nearby bushes. "Here Misty, kitty, kitty, kitty."

"What?" the stranger questioned as he turned his head toward him.

"I was calling the cat. Her name is Misty."

"That's weird. My girlfriend's name is Misty."

"Hmm." He mentally praised himself as he walked away, yet keeping a sly eye on the man who wandered out of sight.

Nick returned to the SUV and briefed his partners on Andy and his words.

William and Travis lifted their binoculars and viewed the apartment.

"She just peeked out," Travis exclaimed, "The curtain moved."

"I saw it too," William replied, "Let's go!"

Ian brushed his teeth before searching the house for his mother; he found her sitting at the kitchen table. "Mom, I just remembered that I had a bad dream last night, I was swimming in the pool and my guardian angel drowned. I tried to save him, but couldn't."

"That is a bad dream." She chuckled to herself. "You know that can't really happen." She motioned for him to near. "Your angel is a spirit. It doesn't have lungs which means it can't even breathe."

"If God tells it to breathe, it can," he stated, waiting for her reply.

"I suppose so, but He wouldn't tell it to."

"Why not?"

"There would be no reason for Him to."

"But He could if He wanted to."

"Yes—God can do anything, except sin."

He thought for a few moments. "Can I go get in the pool?"

"Why?" she asked, "You want to take your guardian angel swimming?"

"Yea."

"You know that your guardian angel is invisible and the water would mean nothing to it."

"It would just fly through the water?" he asked.

"Something like that."

William hammered his fist onto the apartment door. "Come on out Misty, we know you're in there," he yelled, "Swade from Quest Bail Bonds is requiring your presence in Coeur d' Alene."

Travis' heart was pounding as he stood beside his boss and waited for the door to open.

William banged again; the structure remained shut. He stepped back and as he eyed the closed curtains in the window, he lifted his hand to his radio and pushed the talk button. "Any action your way?" he transmitted to Nick who was stationed out back.

"Negative."

"I'm going to go get the landlord. Hold your position, over."

Within the minute, Travis looked across the parking lot and saw that a small crowd was gathering. He became a little nervous as they stared and pointed.

William, who was aggressive and stern, returned within five minutes with the landlord and the key to that apartment. He knocked once again and shouted for Misty. Still, no one opened the door. "We have the key, we're coming in," he warned with a last knock.

Travis radioed to Nick with their intention of entering; to stay on guard.

The apartment supervisor inserted his key into the lock and turned the knob. As he slowly opened the door, he announced his presence. "Hello? It's the landlord!" He stepped in.

William and Travis entered in immediately with their choice of weapon drawn, then William instructed the landlord to wait by the door.

"We're in," Travis conveyed to Nick, "over."

After a quick visual search of the living room and kitchen, William led the way through the dim and quiet hallway. He pointed out a closed door to Travis as he passed by it, then he gestured for him to sift through another room.

Within ten seconds, the rookie exited the bedroom, shaking his head no. He joined William by the closed door.

William grabbed the knob and attempted to turn it, but it was locked. He stepped aside, then yelled, "Misty, come on out. You're going to jail!"

The door stayed at a rest.

"I know you're in there—don't make me break the door down. I'll count to three, then it's coming down." He looked at Travis who was now on the opposite side of the door fame ready and aching to rush in and seize this woman. "One, two, three." He stepped in front of the door, lifted his leg, then the door opened. "Freeze right there." He aimed his pistol at a woman who wasn't Misty.

"Don't shoot!" she appealed as she held up her hands.

"Where's Misty?" he barked.

As she stayed quiet, Travis motioned with his finger for her to walk out of the room to him.

William sped into the bedroom and saw that it was vacant of anyone else. While he cast his eyes about the clutter, he advanced to the closet. He searched the enclosure, then stepped to and looked under the bed. As he returned to a stance, he noticed a large swelling amidst the bedding. Hoping it wasn't just blankets, he smiled to himself, then with Travis again by his side, he lifted the top mattress. "Hello Misty. Did you really think that you were going to get away?"

"Can't blame a girl for trying."

Travis extended his hand to help her to her feet, then he cuffed her.

Reddy and his younger sister Critter hopped into his truck and headed to Kellogg. He needed to replace the blue paint he wasted on his brother. He exited the freeway and traveled south on Hill Street to first drop Critter off at the swimming pool.

"I'll be back in about an hour. I'm gonna go see a friend after I buy the paint," Reddy told her as she withdrew herself from the vehicle.

"No getting high," she replied, "Pa don't like it."

He just smiled as he waved farewell, then drove away toward the hardware store.

"Mom, I'm going to the park to meet Sandy," Nathan spoke as he walked within the kitchen where she was baking and applying frosting to the cup cakes.

"See you at dinner time," she reminded him as he walked out the rear door carrying his backpack.

After a few minutes, he arrived at the park. While he wandered around searching for his friend, he observed children swaying on the swings and others thrusting themselves down the slide. He walked the sidewalk beyond the large fenced swimming pool to the parking lot where he continued to look for Sandy.

"That Bastard! I'm gonna kick his ass if he doesn't show up," Nathan spoke to himself, then returned to the pool area. He sat on a bench and watched the swimmers.

Outfitted in a yellow bikini, Critter climbed the pool ladder to the cement ground, then lifted her arms to wring the water from her long wet hair.

Nathan opened his mouth in awe and with his wide brown eyes, he gazed at the beautiful curves of this girl.

Critter released her hair and stepped toward the fence. "Hi Nathan," she expressed softly as she smiled at him.

"Hi," he replied in a reserved manner.

"Are you coming swimming?"

"No."

She eyed his backpack that lay on the bench beside him. "You have a soccer game?"

"No. I'm suppose to be meeting a friend," he explained, "but he hasn't showed up yet."

She thought for a moment. "I'll come out there and sit by you while you wait, okay?"

"Yea." He watched her turn and walk away. What was up with this hot-ass girl, he thought, and why would she want to talk to me?

Dominique and Ian were done swimming in their indoor pool. They wrapped a towel around themselves and went to their separate bedrooms to change out the their wet suits.

After she entered her room and locked the door, she stepped to her dresser and pushed the play button on her compact disc player, letting the music transmit through the air.

Matt who was shirtless, advanced into the room from their master bath just as his wife slipped her sports bra off. "Mmm." His face brightened when he saw her hard nipples. "You know, we haven't done it since I came home."

She was smitten. He hardly ever approached her. "Yea?" she urged, waiting for him to make the move as she patted herself with the towel.

He moved in behind her, coiled his arms around to her front side, and cupped his masculine hands onto her breasts. "They're cold."

She giggled. "Of course they are. I just went swimming." She withdrew her wet shorts down to her ankles.

As she bent, a glimpse of her heaven sent him into a state of passion. He quickly downed his pants and pressed his naked body onto hers. "I love you," he whispered with courage, then positioned her over the bed for his pleasure.

After Matt and Dominique were done coming together, they dressed and sat together upon their bed. He lit a joint, inhaled and held it for five seconds, then blew it out. "I want you to know why I went to Arizona."

"I already have an idea why," she stated as she took hold of the marijuana stick.

"I found her!" His hazel eyes widened with excitement. "I wanted to tell you last night, but other things came first." He glanced at the wedding ring on his finger.

"Tell me about her."

"She looks like Nisa. She's engaged to a guy named Adam. He use to be a cadet in the police academy, but dropped out. They're coming up to Idaho at the end of the week; I want to train him to be a bounty hunter."

"Sounds like a good idea."

"They need a place to stay so I was hoping they could stay here while they look for an apartment?" He looked into her blue eyes with much anticipation.

She really didn't like strangers to live in her house, but her Christian hospitality set in so she pushed her selfish nature aside. "They could stay in the guest room."

Nathan had butterflies fluttering around in his stomach as Critter approached the bench where he was sitting. She was arrayed in a white and flowery sundress and she wore sandals on her feet. He observed that her toenails were painted purple to match the flowers on her dress.

She sat down on the bench with the backpack between them. "I love the summertime—it's so romantic."

"Yea, I guess." He wanted to turn his head and stare at her, but he knew that would be too immature so he just glanced, then glanced again.

"Any sign of your friend yet?"

"No."

There was a pause.

"I could have my brother drive us around town to look for him," she suggested, "He'll be here soon to pick me up."

"Maybe," he replied. "How many brothers do you have?"

"Two. Reddy and Luke Junior, but we just call him Luke cuz we call our dad, Pa."

He thought that was weird to call your dad Pa.

"What about you, your family?" she asked.

"I have three brothers and a mom."

"No dad?"

"No. He died when I was seven."

"How odd is that? My mom died when I was seven."

"That is odd."

Critter cast her vision to the parking lot and saw Reddy walking up the sidewalk toward them. "My brother's here," she announced as she glanced at Nathan, then stood to her feet and waved her arm to get her sibling's attention. She returned to the bench while she waited for him to near.

Nathan noted Reddy's height to be about six feet and his muscles were more exposed than his own.

"Ready to go little sis?" Reddy asked as he stopped at the bench.

"Yea. Can we drive around on a few streets to look for Sandy, Nathan's friend?"

"Is this Nathan?" He motioned his head toward Nathan.

"Yea. He's my new friend."

"Sure—let's go."

Nathan grabbed his backpack and strolled with Critter to their truck. He set his baggage in the bed next to a container of paint.

Reddy drove east on McKinley Avenue to South Main, ending up on Division Street. With no sign of Nathan's friend, he turned around and headed back toward the town center.

"So Nathan," Reddy broke the silence. "What do you do?"

"Nothing too much." Not sure of what he meant, he continued. "I'm thinking about being a volunteer for the fire crew."

"What kind of crap is that?"

"Volunteer may be the wrong word. I would sign up in the program and it does pay," he defended.

"I'm just flipping you shit. How old are you?"

"Seventeen."

"He plays on a soccer team," Critter inserted, "I watched him play and he's pretty good."

Nathan gleamed within himself.

Reddy steered his truck into the parking lot of the grocery store. "We need some food. Will you go in Critter?" He advanced into a space on the far side of the building and parked.

"I guess so." She exited the truck with a hundred dollars, then stepped in view of the open passenger window. "Will you still be out here when I get done shopping?" she asked Nathan.

"Yes," Reddy quickly answered as he leaned forward against the steering wheel and looked at her. "He's gonna sit out here and talk to me."

She sent her brother a dirty look before turning and walking toward the store entrance. She knew he would cause trouble whether it was on purpose or unknowingly.

Reddy cast his vision onto Nathan who was sitting quiet. "So Nathan—Do you smoke weed?"

He expressed interest as he looked at him. "I've smoked a couple of times."

"You want a few tokes?"

"Sure."

Reddy took a joint out of his cigarette pack and handed it to his guest. "Keep it low."

Nathan lit the tip and inhaled. He tried to pass it to Reddy, but he declined. "No—go ahead," he replied, "I'm already baked!"

He inhaled another lung full of smoke.

Reddy extracted a cigarette from his pack. "Uh-oh . . ." He realized that he had given him the wrong joint. Nathan was smoking on the marijuana stick that had been dipped in PCP. After a third toke, Reddy suggested he give the joint back.

Critter soon returned to the truck pushing a cart full of grocery bags. Reddy hopped out of his vehicle and while he loaded their edibles into the bed of the truck, she stepped to the passenger door to open it and saw Nathan sitting in a stupor. "Nathan?" She stared at him with wonder.

He slowly turned his face to her and gave a lazy smile.

She observed his bloodshot eyes and sluggish condition. "Are you okay?"

"I'm looking for my friend Sandy," he spoke slow, "Have you seen him?"

"No," she answered softly, then cast her eyes to her brother. "What did you give him?"

He leaned toward her. "I just gave him a few tokes," he whispered.

"Of what?" she scolded in a low tone. "He looks totally out of it."

"Just get in the truck," he ordered, "And scoot him over so he's in between us." He gyrated and hustled to his side of the truck where he jumped into the driver's seat. He started the engine, backed out of the parking space, and sped away.

"I'm not feeling very well," Nathan disclosed as he rubbed his sweaty palms together.

"Where do you live?" Critter asked her companion.

"With my mom."

"I'm not taking him home!" Reddy abruptly proclaimed, "I'll just take him home with us." He flipped on the turn signal and after steering onto the freeway ramp, he accelerated.

Within a few minutes, Reddy began to sing a jest. "On the good ship, lollipop is a SWEET TRIP . . ."

"That's not funny!" Critter rebuked.

CHAPTER FIVE

The Next Day

Dominique paced the floor most of the night, staying close to the telephone. Her thoughts were of her under aged son who hadn't come home for dinner the previous evening. She pondered on where he could have gone to and why. Could he have ran away? She asked herself, then quickly threw that possibility out of her brain because she knew there would be no reason for him to; they had a good mother-son relationship. Her worst fear would be of him being kidnapped, tortured, and killed. She wiped the tears from her face and told herself to not think of such horrible things.

She butted her cigarette into the already full ashtray, arose from her swing chair, and returned to the inside of her house. She placed her hand onto her chest and coughed. She was starting to hurt from too much smoking.

Matt entered into the kitchen where Dominique was arranging raw cinnamon dough into tin pans. "Did he come home?"

"No," she answered, then yawned.

"I think maybe we should go search Sandy's house. He probably got really drunk and didn't want to come home."

"I don't know Matt. Sandy sounded sincere on the telephone last night when he said he hadn't seen him all of yesterday."

"Teenagers lie Dominique," he stated.

"We could drive up there after these cinnamon rolls are done. And if there's no sign of him, I'm going to the police station."

Nathan opened his crusty eyelids and observed that he was in an unfamiliar environment. Photographs of strangers were spread about the shelves, as well as odd pieces of knickknacks and books. The smell of old house drifted about the dusty, dim lighted living room. "Where the fuck am I?" he asked himself as he sat up from a shabby blue couch.

He felt pain within his head while he examined himself to make sure he was okay as well as dressed. He wiped his eyes and waited for his vision to come to full focus, then stepped to the shelves where he got a closer look at the photos. He recognized a few to be Critter.

He tried to remember how he arrived there at her house. He recalled looking for Sandy after sitting at the park with Critter, then he remembered smoking pot with Reddy. "That was a powerful joint!" he whispered.

Nathan went to the front interior door of the house. He looked out the small window and saw Reddy's white truck parked in the gravel driveway. He cast his eyes about and observed a small grassy yard surrounded by pine trees; lots of pine trees. He noted a scanty dirt lane that quickly vanished within the forest of bushes and sorts of trees. "I'm out in the freakin boonies," he spoke low to himself, afraid of what may come.

He turned around and walked toward and through the threshold of the kitchen. He noted the clean, but old appliances and counters as he advanced quietly to search for a bathroom.

After finding and using the toilet, he downed a few aspirins from the medicine cabinet, then returned to the kitchen where he encountered Critter's presence. "Hi," he expressed with a hint of shyness.

She repaid the greeting with a smile.

"I need to go home," he told her.

"You'll have to wait until Reddy wakes up."

"Do you have a phone so I could call my mom? She's probably worried about me."

"My other brother Luke has a cell phone, but he's out of minutes right now," she replied, "And when he does have minutes, he has to climb to the roof of the house to even get one bar."

He smiled. "That's funny."

"You want some breakfast?" she asked him as she removed the eggs and a package of sausage from the refrigerator.

"Yea, sounds good." Nathan sat himself on a chair at the kitchen table and spied her figure through the pink cotton shorts and t-shirt she was wearing. "So what do you do if you have an emergency? I mean with no telephone."

She turned and cast her pure blue eyes upon him. "My brother has a gun."

He gulped.

The smell of food cooking aroused Reddy and Luke from their bunks and from their bedroom. Critter was serving Nathan when they stepped into the kitchen with cigarettes in between their lips.

Nathan felt odd eating in front of them, especially Luke who he hadn't met yet, he thought, or at least he didn't remember meeting him, but figured he was Reddy's twin brother.

Critter sat on the chair next to Nathan with her plate of eggs and sausage. "Nathan wants a ride home," she disclosed as she watched her brother.

Reddy blew his draw of smoke out to his side. "Later."

After Dominique took her morning shower, she dialed her oldest son at his home to inform him of her plans about Nathan, then scampered up the staircase to Travis' bedroom to ask him if he'd stay with Ian for a few hours and sit by the telephone.

Just when Matt was reversing his Explorer from the driveway, Nick arrived in his own truck, stopping suddenly at the curb. Dominique poked her head out the passenger's side window at him.

"I'll follow you," Nick shouted to his mom, "I want to help find my brother."

They drove through Kellogg, up Main Street to Wardner until they came to Sandy's house.

Sandy's mother opened the door and confirmed that Nathan hadn't been there.

"May I speak with Sandy?" Dominique asked.

"Come on in."

Dominique, Matt, and Nick entered her house and waited by the door while she fetched her son from his second floor bedroom. A minute later, she returned with Sandy.

"You look tired?" Dominique remarked with curiosity as he neared.

"I've been working on my lego ship all night."

"Alone?"

"Yea. Nathan never showed up."

"Do you know of any other friend he may have hooked up with?"

Sandy moved his head slowly from side to side as he gave thought.

"Will you show us where the Glen is?"

"I guess so. You think he's up there?"

"It's worth a look," she replied.

He slipped his boots on and left with the concerned trio. He rode with Nick down the inclining road and around the small mountain into Kellogg.

Matt followed behind on a paved lane that was constructed on the edge of the mountainside. When the road came to a dead end, they parked and exited their vehicles.

Sandy led the way. He started out on a grassy trail that became rockier and steeper as they hiked the hillside. They soon arrived at the boys' fort; an old abandoned water reservoir. Sandy advanced onto a plank and with the aid of his hands, he ascended the board until he reached the top. He then stepped onto the cement wall, turned his upper body around, and waved them up.

Nick went first, then Dominique. By the time Matt surfaced, Sandy had the trap door open and was stepping down the ladder that led into the small concrete structure.

Sandy scanned the area. "I don't think he's been here," he stated to Nick as he watched Dominique and Matt descend from the wall ladder.

Nick stepped to their homemade fireplace and eyed the setup. "Awesome little fort," he praised, "I'm impressed."

Matt looked at Sandy. "You could probably get into trouble for trespassing," he kindly added, "If you get caught."

Dominique cast her eyes about the enclosure. She noted two old couch cushions lying on the cement floor that Nathan and Sandy used to sit on while they sat around the fire and ate or smoked cigarettes. There was a small pile of firewood, a pan for cooking, and food wrappers scattered about.

Matt soon approached his wife. "Are you ready to go?"

She looked upon him with a worried countenance. "Where could he be?"

He just shrugged his shoulders as he replied, "I don't know, he's your son."

"That was a cold thing to say."

"I only meant that you know him better than I know him."

Nathan was perched on the main sofa with Reddy playing one of his favorite video games, hence his mind was distracted from wanting to go home. He pressed the A button and moved the thumb stick up on his controller which caused his quarterback to throw the football to a wide receiver who then ran it for a touchdown. "Yah!" he cheered, "I win."

"Yes, you did," Reddy agreed sadly as he set his control device on the coffee table. He returned his backside to the couch, then stretched and yawned. "I guess it's time to start on the back yard," he expressed his displeasure to Nathan.

"What do you have to do to the back yard?" he asked.

"Clean it up. Pa wants it to look like the Garden of Eden."

Luke entered into the living room carrying a duffel bag.

"Where are you going?" Reddy asked his twin with a curious stare.

"I'm bored. I'm going to Susie Parker's house for a few days."

"Yea—bored my ass!" Reddy jested, "You're horny."

Luke Junior grinned as he headed for the door.

"What about the back yard?" he called out.

"Get Nathan to help you."

Reddy turned to Nathan. "I think we need to get stoned before we start on the yard."

"We? I need to go home," he replied.

"Might as well stay for a while and help. You're probably in trouble anyways, right?"

"I'll be grounded for the rest of the summer."

"Make it worth your while then." He removed from the cubby drawer in the coffee table, his tray of marijuana.

Critter entered the room and sat in the easy chair with her book. Nathan eyed her as he reflected on what Reddy had just said about making his stay worth while. He gave thought to how he wanted to keep watching Critter, kiss her small inviting lips, and eventually do her.

"Besides," Reddy interrupted his daydream as he loaded the pipe, "You have to stay now. Luke just drove away in the truck."

While Nick took Sandy home, Matt and Dominique drove to their estate to see if Nathan had come home. With no sign of him, they left again in their truck and headed to the local park where they searched on foot.

They were soon on their way to the police station. Matt parked his vehicle and they walked inside the brick building.

"How long has it been since you last seen him?" the husky Latin American officer asked the worried mother from across the counter.

"It's been twenty-four hours. He left yesterday around noon to go meet his friend at the park."

"Have you talked to his friend since then?"

"Yes." Dominique answered firmly as she eyed him. "Of course I talked to him. Then I spoke with his mother and I even went up to their house to verify that he wasn't there. Sandy said he didn't meet Nathan yesterday because he fell asleep."

"What about family members? Grandparents . . ."

"I hadn't really thought of that yet." She moved her eyes about as she processed her thoughts. "He never sees them, but if he did, I know he would call me." She returned her vision upon the policeman.

"Why don't you check with them first, then come back if you still need to file a report," he suggested.

An hour had passed by when Dominique and Matt returned to the Kellogg police station with negative results from certain relatives and a photo of Nathan. She watched the officer fill out the report as he asked questions.

"No—no birthmarks or tattoos," she claimed.

"What was he wearing?"

"Blue sports shorts, a blue and white jersey, and blue and white sneakers."

"He must like blue," the cop remarked.

She gave a weary smile.

"I think that's all I need right now. I'll get this information out over the wire," he spoke with a grave expression on his face. "We'll be looking for your son."

"Thank you." She and Matt turned and left the station.

When they arrived home, she scampered up the staircase to Nathan's bedroom where she spied for clues. She stepped to his bureau and saw his wallet lying there. She lifted and opened it. His identification and social security card were in place as well as a few photos. She noted a twenty dollar bill in the side aperture and next to it was an unused condom. "Eww!" She folded and set the wallet back onto the dresser.

Travis and Ian entered the room. "Anything missing?"

"No," she answered with a glance. "His clothes are all here, his wallet's here. Just his backpack, cd player, and cd's are gone." She advanced to and sat on his bed. She bowed her head and covered her face as she began to sob. "Where could he be? My Louy-Spouy."

"It's still early Mom," Travis tried to comfort her. "We'll find him—The Underdog bounty hunters are on it."

She laid back on his bed and wrapped her arm around his pillow. "I'm so tired." She yawned and closed her teary eyes.

CHAPTER SIX

A Few Fliers

The next morning, Dominique was up early tending to the laundry. She was also fitting the spare bedroom for Rainy and Adam's arrival. She applied clean sheets to the double sized bed, spread out a blanket, then arranged a comforter across the bed, covering the two new pillows that she had purchased for them. She dusted the bureau and end tables. Last of all, she vacuumed the light blue carpet.

Matt stepped into the laundry room with a bowl of weed and sat on the bench. "You want a few tokes?" he asked his wife who was now folding towels.

"Maybe one or two. I have stuff to do today."

"Like what?"

She cast an odd look his way. "Are you for real? My son is missing. I'm going to go make up fliers and search for him."

"I'll help."

The telephone rang. Matt arose from the bench and exited the room to answer it. He soon returned to his wife. "Travis and I have to go into the office this morning, but I'll still help you this afternoon." He grabbed his pipe and kissed her good bye.

Dominique went to her home office and sat at her desk. She took hold of a five by seven photo of Nathan and taped it to a piece of typing paper, then with her marker, she wrote the necessary information below the photo, including a ten thousand dollar reward.

After freshening up, she and Ian left the house and went on their way to the Uptown Print Shop where she had them print five hundred copies.

"Mom—Are we gonna find Nathan?" Ian asked as they approached their car.

"We're going to put the word out, maybe someone has seen him."

"Is he dead?"

"No!" she quickly answered, "Don't say that."

"I miss him. He use to jump on the trampoline with me."

"I miss him too Baby Zebra." She lit a cigarette and accelerated. Within two minutes, she was parked at the grocery store, beginning her search as she and Ian stood in front of the building, passing out fliers and periodically talking to people.

Matt and Travis eyed the marker board that William was using to write descriptions of their next bounty. They tried to pay close attention, but with Nathan missing, their minds drifted back and forth.

"Gary is five foot six, a hundred and ninety pounds, brown curly hair and blue eyes."

"A short, plump guy," Travis commented.

"Yes," William replied, "You can see that from his photo. You can also see that he likes bling."

They viewed the print.

"Which brings us to my plan," he continued as he cast his thought upon Travis. "How good are you at lying?"

"I can do it," he spoke with confidence, wanting to prove his skills.

"Okay—we need to draw this criminal out, quickly and easily. Call Gary, tell him you're from Brass' Jewelry—he won a prize."

Sitting at William's desk, Travis scooted the telephone back his way and as he stared at it, he inhaled a deep breath and let it out.

"I know I can easily do this myself," William stated to his rookie, "but I wanted to give you some training in this field."

"Don't be nervous," Matt encouraged his step son.

Travis dialed the number to Gary's home phone and waited for an answer.

"Hello?" a rough voice came over the wire.

"Hello. Am I speaking with Gary?"

"Could be. Who is this?"

"Who is this you ask?" he spoke in a goofy manner, "This is your local jeweler calling to let you know that you've won our grand prize from our drawing and you have just one hour to come into the store and claim it or it goes to the runner-up."

Matt and William smiled at each other.

"Whad I win?"

"A sterling silver necklace valued at nearly two hundred dollars."

"Nice." He paused a moment. "I didn't put my name in any drawing."

"Well someone did Gary! Maybe your mother, maybe your girlfriend?"

"Maybe."

Travis ended the call and after he returned the receiver to the base, William congratulated him on a job well done. "Now we need to get ourselves uptown and stake it out. You two gear up in the SUV while I drive." The Underdogs hustled out of the office carrying their implements, William locked the door, and they dashed for the vehicle.

Once uptown, William parked across the street from Brass' Jewelry. Matt walked to the street corner bench and sat while Travis went inside the store. After talking with the employee, he roamed the establishment, waiting for their culprit.

Some thirty minutes later, Gary was seen strolling near the jewelry store. "He's at the display window," William transmitted to Matt and Travis. "Make a positive identification before confirming and approaching," he told Travis. "Matt, wait until he enters the store to get up and follow. I'll then join you."

Travis stood behind a display case in order to conceal his armor. While Gary stepped toward the salesclerk, he observed his posture and facial features, then quietly radioed to his partners for immediate back-up.

After Gary advanced to the counter, to the employee and told her he was there for his prize, she pointed to Travis. He turned himself around and saw the strange man standing three feet away, dangling a pair of handcuffs in front of him.

"Put your hands behind your back!" Travis ordered.

"Shit," he spoke low with confusion, then hastened toward the door.

Travis gave chase.

Matt and William entered through the door of the jewelry store and unexpectedly collided into Gary. Gary bounced back.

"You hold it right there mother fucker!" William scolded as he forced Gary face down on the counter and cuffed him. "If you don't go to court, you go back to jail!"

"And who are you?" he roared.

"A personal friend of Swade's."

William dropped Matt off at the Underdog's office, then with Travis' guard on Gary, he drove to Coeur d' Alene to surrender his prisoner to the county jail.

Matt removed and locked up his gear in his locker before leaving in his truck for the grocery store to meet up with Dominique.

After he parked in a space next to her car, he observed her and Ian walking towards him. "Having any luck?" he asked her as he stepped out of his vehicle.

"Nope. Nobody's seen him."

He cast his eyes upon the box of fliers that was placed upon the front seat in her car. "How many have you passed out?"

"About a hundred. Are you still gonna help me?"

"Yea."

She retrieved and handed him a portion of the fliers. "How'd your bounty go?"

"We got him! He was an easy catch."

"Good for you," she replied, then lit a cigarette. "I'm going to go uptown to the newspaper office and pay to have them run this in tomorrow's paper."

Matt soon left in his Explorer and drove around town, taping or tacking fliers to bulletin boards or windows of a few businesses, but mostly the taverns.

He entered Swiner's Pub and walked with slack to the bar. He sat onto a stool and as he waited for the bartender, he felt a sensation of dryness in his mouth. He licked his parched lips and gave thought to ordering a beer, but he knew he shouldn't.

When Dominique took Ian home for a late lunch, an unfamiliar car with two strangers sitting inside on the two front seats was parked alongside the curb. They went into their house and shut the door. She stepped into the kitchen and after gathering sandwich fixings from the refrigerator, she heard a knock at the door. "Dang it!" she mumbled, then looked at Ian. "You'll have to make your own sandwich." She exhaled a long deep breath. "Maybe they know where Nathan is." She left the kitchen, advanced to and opened the anterior door.

"Good afternoon Ma'am," one of the two men bid as they presented badges. "May we come in?"

"Yes." She widened the door, then they entered.

"We have a search warrant."

"Why?" she asked in awe.

"It's procedure to do so when a family member comes up missing," the special agent explained, "Foul play usually starts within the family."

She dispatched a scornful look his way. "Nobody in my family would hurt Nathan or even think about it!"

"I'm sure that's the case." He held up his broad hand in defense. "We still have to investigate."

"You didn't need a search warrant. I would of let you come in and look." She took in a large breath and exhaled. She knew this was nonsense and a waste of time.

"Now . . . will you show us Nathan's bedroom?"

Matt ordered his third beer as well as a drink for his buddy who wandered into the establishment a beer ago. They talked of his bounty hunting business, Trevor's work, then of Nathan. Matt mentioned how he was out and about distributing fliers.

The two drunkards were soon playing pool. Their first game led to a second and during that, a group of three strolled into the tavern and took control of the other billiard table.

Matt eyed the blonde as she stepped about with her large breasts and bent in for her table shots. As he stood waiting for Trevor to make his play, he looked down at his left hand and inconspicuously twisted his ring off.

Trevor sank the eight ball and won the game, making the score one to one.

"Two out of three," Matt urged as he slipped his wedding band into his jeans pocket.

"Shouldn't you get going . . . go help your wife pass out fliers?"

"There's still time." He glanced at the blonde who was out of ear range.

"Okay—let's play."

Matt inserted two quarters into the coin guide to release the balls, then he racked them.

Trevor broke, scattering the balls which caused one of the solids to drop down a pocket. He took another shot and missed.

After Matt took his turn, the beautiful woman advanced his way and spoke, "Nice shot, you play very well."

"Thank you," he responded with a grin. "I've had lots of practice."

She returned the smile.

"What's your name?"

"Jamie."

"Hi Jamie," he whispered in a charming way close to her ear. "Can I buy you a drink?" He suddenly turned his upper torso about when he felt the presence of someone standing behind him.

"What's going on?" A tough looking fellow asked.

The woman turned too. "Oh . . . Ricky. I was just telling this guy he plays very well."

He cast a glare on Matt. "It didn't look that way to me."

Matt stepped back. "That's what happened." He then walked around the pool table to take his shot while keeping an eye on Ricky who was now guiding his woman to her chair. With his next turn, he scratched on purpose, losing the game. "I'll see you later Trevor." He returned the cue to its rack, took two gulps of his beer, and left the pub.

He drove to another tavern and after tacking a flier to the bulletin board, he sat at the bar and ordered a beer.

Dominique was mentally exhausted after an afternoon of questions from the two detectives. She lit a cigarette and plopped herself onto an easy chair in the living room, then glanced at her watch. "Where the heck is Matt?" She thought he would of only been an hour or two. She arose from her chair to cast a peek at the empty driveway from her bay window, then began to feel her stomach grumbling. She hadn't eaten all day.

She went to the kitchen and made herself a sandwich. After eating, she sat with a joint on the broad ledge of the bay window and waited for her husband.

Within the hour, Matt arrived home.

She noted he had parked crooked; the front tire was partially on the lawn. As she watched him stagger up the sidewalk, her insides filled with disappointment. When he entered into the house, he acted as though he didn't see her. He walked unsteadily to their master bedroom. She followed him.

Dominique was perched upon her bed when he exited the lavatory. He stood in the center of their bedroom and looked at her with a blank face.

"Aren't you going to talk to me?" she asked.

"What do you want me to say?" he slurred.

She exhibited shock from his question. "Ask me how my afternoon went. Tell me what you did." She raised her voice. "Don't just ignore me cuz you're stinkin' drunk!"

He sat down on his chair. "I passed out a few fliers," he replied calmly as he took off his shoes.

"Where's your ring?"

He was speechless as he slowly lowered his vision to his hand.

Dominique stormed out of her bedroom and went outside to Matt's truck. She scanned the cab for any remnants of infidelity. She picked up the pile of fliers she had given to him earlier and estimated. "He only passed out four or five."

Luke Junior drove his truck upon the shady lane to his home. After parking, he carried his duffel bag inside and searched for Reddy. In the kitchen, he encountered his sister. "Hi Critter." He patted the five foot three girl atop of her head with his free hand. "Smells good in here, like cinnamon."

"I'm making an apple pie. Nathan said he hasn't eaten one in a while."

"Mm-hm. I like apple pie too. When's the last time you made one for me?"

She returned his smile. "Nathan's cuter, but you can still have a piece of this one."

"Where's Reddy?"

"He's in the back yard."

Luke took his duffel bag to his bedroom before stepping out onto the back porch. "Hey brother!" he called.

"Hey!" Reddy greeted as he looked his way, then advanced to him. "Have a good time with Susie?"

"A terrific time," he spoke, then released the grin from his face. "I need to talk to you." He observed Nathan as he came near. "Privately."

"Take a break Nathan, I'll be right back," Reddy imposed, then followed Luke to their shared bedroom.

Luke closed the door. "You need to take Nathan home."

"Why?"

"Because his disappearance is all over the news! You could get into big trouble." He reached into his duffel bag, pulled out the day's newspaper, and opened it to the correct page.

CHAPTER SEVEN

A Diversion

Reddy crumpled the newspaper article after reading it, then shoved it into his top dresser drawer. "He's staying!" he expressed his demand to his brother who was sitting on his bed. "I still want his help with the yard while I come up with a plan."

"A plan?" Luke wore concern upon his face. "You can't keep him!"

"Yes I can," he replied.

Dominique and Ian finished their water exercises and left the natatorium. They went to their bedrooms to change clothes before meeting again in the kitchen for lunch. While they ate their chicken salads, Matt entered in and quietly stepped to the refrigerator for a soda.

There was a knock at the front door. When Matt opened the entry way, his niece and her fiance' were standing there. "Rainy—Adam, come on in." After he moved the door aside to let them enter, he gave Rainy a quick hug and Adam a handshake. "I'm glad you're here. How'd the trip up go?"

"Great. We stopped at the Grand Canyon for one night," Adam spoke.

"Never been there, but I hear it's a big place!" Matt jested.

"We also stopped over at the Crystal Ice Cave near American Falls. Now that was beautiful."

"Yea," Rainy continued, "It has a frozen river and a frozen waterfall."

"I'm gonna have to go there someday."

Dominique stepped into the living room and approached the trio with a smile. "This must be Rainy and Adam. It's nice to finally meet you two." She shook their hands.

"It's nice to meet you too," Rainy spoke timidly.

"Well—your room is all ready for you. I can show you around my estate now if you'd like."

"Yes, I need to walk around. My rear end is sore from sitting."

While the men brought in the luggage from Adam's car, Dominique led the way through her large house showing Rainy the kitchen, her and Adam's bedroom and bathroom, then the indoor pool.

"Sweet. I can use this anytime I want?"

"Yes. I just have one basic rule. No peeing or spitting."

"Oh . . . of course not. That's gross."

Nathan released a long, loud burp. "Not bad manners, but good apple pie," he remarked to Critter as he winked at her.

With a touch of shyness, she smiled at him, then arose from her kitchen chair, took hold of their plates, and carried them to the sink.

He stood to his feet and stretched.

Critter stepped close to him. "Do you want to go to my secret getaway place now?"

"Sure."

She peeked into the living room to see that Luke and Reddy were fully engrossed with their Alienoids video game, then turned and gestured for Nathan to follow her.

He followed her back through the kitchen, through the hallway, and into her bedroom. "I don't think I should be in your bedroom. Your brother's might not like it."

She closed the door. "Don't be silly, we're not staying in here." She grabbed a small purse and stuffed it into her pocket before stepping to her window. She lifted the pane and climbed onto the ledge.

"Where are you going?" he asked as he advanced to her.

"Up." She scaled a ladder that was attached to the exterior side of the house.

Nathan pursued her. He entered through a small door just under the overhang of the roof and as he cast his eyes about the attic, he smelled a stale odor. A miniature table with a teapot and toy cups lay scattered atop and there were dolls sitting in each of the three chairs.

"I haven't been up here in a while," she claimed.

"It's a nice little fort. Me and Sandy have a fort in the mountains. We call it The Glen." As he told her more of it, he observed a picture of a naked man posted on a nearby beam.

Critter stepped to the beam and quickly ripped the obscenity from his view. "Sorry about that," she apologized with a hint of embarrassment.

"Does Luke and Reddy know about this little getaway place?"

"Yea, but they haven't been up here in years. It's mostly my place." She pulled the little purse from her pocket, sat on the dusty floor, and invited Nathan to join her. She opened the pouch and withdrew a pipe and a plastic bag.

Nathan's eyes widened. "You smoke pot?"

"Don't tell my brothers."

He watched her with interest as she loaded the bowl and took the first toke. He silently ogled over her slender pink lips, her petite nose, and her smooth unblemished skin. He became aware of and caught some drool with his tongue before she looked up at him and passed the pipe. He inhaled and held the smoke for a few moments, then exhaled. "I'm curious Critter, where are we?"

"In the deep, deep forest of Idaho."

He became confused, wondering about her mentality. "I mean, what's the closest city or town from here?"

"I know we go through Pinehurst, but that's miles and miles away." She took in a second toke and let it out. "Don't you like being here with me?"

"Yea, I do."

"So you're not going home yet?" She popped out her lower lip, showing sorrow.

"I have to go home soon." He scooted closer to her. "But we can enjoy the time we have now."

"That's so sweet."

He moved his index finger and thumb to her chin and tilted her face upwards, leaned in and kissed her.

"Critter!?"

Their kiss was broken at the sound of Reddy's voice calling from her open bedroom window.

Nathan took one last quick puff from the pipe before stuffing it into the purse.

Critter stood and walked to the small attic door. "What do you want?" She looked down at her brother.

"What are you doing?"

"I'm showing Nathan my fort."

"He's seen it—now come down!"

"In our location we have to deal with both Idaho and Washington," Matt explained to Adam while Rainy and Dominique listened. "There's no regulations in Idaho, but for Washington you have to be certified and licensed. There's a three day class that starts on Monday. I already signed you up for it."

"Sweet! Thank you boss," Adam replied, "Now these classes are for what exactly?"

"Use of force, hand gun qualification, taser and pepper spray, umm ... the clearing of a building or room. And after you pass the exam," he continued, "we'll fit you in your gear."

Dominique arose from the couch with boredom. She went to her bedroom and soon returned into the living room with Ian trailing behind. "I'll be back later." She patted Matt on the shoulder as she headed for the door. Once outside, she and Ian climbed into her car and drove away.

"Where are we going Mom?"

"Just for a drive."

"To search for Nathan?"

She looked his way and answered him with sadness in her voice. "Yea." She steered her vehicle onto the freeway ramp and accelerated—her aim was Pinehurst.

Matt and his two house guests went outside. He was the only one smoking as they talked.

Travis came jogging down the staircase, dashed out the front door, and headed for his truck.

"Where ya going Travis?" Matt questioned.

"The gym. I have to go tone my bounty hunting arms."

"Can I go with you?" Adam called out.

"Sure. Come on." He waved him over, presuming he was Adam, the new trainee.

Adam addressed Rainy with a kiss and hurried to the truck. As they drove away, he held his arm up near the open window and flexed his muscle as to impress her.

She giggled.

There was a moment of silence before Matt asked her what she wanted to do with her life.

"I want to be a veterinarian."

"Wow. How long do you have to go to school to do that?"

"Eight years."

"Dang! That's as long as a people doctor. You'll be about . . . twenty six when you graduate?"

"Yea, but it'll be worth it. I'll have a high paying job and I love animals."

He thought for a moment as he puffed on his cigarette. "There's an animal clinic here in Kellogg. Maybe you could help wash animals or something until you start school," he suggested.

"Maybe—Uncle Matt."

Nathan and Critter walked into the living room; one sat in the easy chair, the other onto the love seat.

Luke Junior and Reddy were on level three of their video game when Reddy pushed pause and peered at Nathan. "The back yard ain't gonna do itself."

Both Luke and Critter sat quiet as they turned their attention to Nathan.

Nathan was momentarily struck speechless by the remark, but quickly threw it aside. "No it ain't—so you should get out there."

Reddy glared at him and with the raise of his voice, he spoke. "Get out there or I'll beat you like a red-headed stepchild!" He then smiled at him. "Just kidding." He dangled a joint. "I'll smoke this with you, then you'll go saw down those branches?"

"Sure," he replied after feeling threatened.

"I'll help you Nathan," Critter offered.

Reddy interfered. "Don't you have to start supper?"

"You start supper you bossy jerk!" she roared as she stood to her feet, then stormed off.

He looked at Nathan. "Don't worry about her, she gets like that sometimes."

"Probably premenstrual," Luke added.

Nathan didn't say a word even though he agreed with Critter.

Reddy went to his bedroom, opened his dresser drawer, and took hold of the crumpled newspaper. He unfolded and tried to smooth out the wrinkles so he could read the article thoroughly. "A reward huh? It's tempting," he spoke to himself, "but I wouldn't get it. Nathan would tell them I kidnapped him." He set the newspaper next to him on the bed and gave thought to a plan of keeping his thrall.

Luke came into the bedroom and joined his brother. "Did you read the report on page two?"

"No, I didn't read it." He picked up the paper and turned to the appropriate page.

"They say they have a witness who saw Nathan walking around Pinehurst with a group of teenagers and a few of them live in Pinecreek so they may get close."

"You know it's a false witness."

"We know that—but not the detectives." He paused. "What you need to do is create a diversion so that the authorities look for Nathan somewhere totally opposite of our area."

"But where?" Reddy asked.

"Send them on a wild-goose chase. Say . . . Wallace or Mullan."

"And then what? What I'm mostly concerned about is the end result. He's been here only a week and that's enough time for them to convict me."

"You should of already taken him home."

"I know—I know, but I didn't."

"Well . . . try to thwart the authorities, then think of how you're going to take care of this end result and do it before Pa gets home."

That evening when Nathan was in the shower, Reddy went through his backpack to see if there was anything that would identify him. With no luck, he dumped the contents of the backpack onto the blue couch, then took it to the kitchen where he wrote Nathan's name on the inside. He hurried through the living room, quickly telling Luke he'd be home later, then scampered out the door with the backpack.

"Where's he goin'?" Critter asked Luke from the easy chair.

"To town."

"He'd better pick up some milk."

Reddy drove about twelve miles to the town of Pinehurst. He traveled amongst the collection of buildings and past the crowded police station before coming to the freeway. He accelerated on the ramp to full speed, heading due east and soon by-passed Kellogg and advanced to the historical town of Wallace.

Upon arriving in Wallace, he left the expressway, crossed over a scant bridge, and turned onto the I-90 business loop. After driving only a few yards, he quickly steered into a gas station and parked around back beside a dumpster. He gave thought to where he could leave the orange bag for the authorities to find. He eyed the outside of the large garbage bin as a possibility, but decided against it. "Someone would just throw it away."

He shifted into first gear and sped away. He drove into the small town as far as Bank Street, the main drag. He slowed his vehicle and looked for an open space to deposit his truck, then he parked parallel in front of a hardware store. He shut off the engine and scanned the area. There were few people walking the sidewalk on both sides of the street. "If I could blend in," he said to himself, "and drop the bag as I pass by . . ."

Reddy exited his truck carrying Nathan's backpack. He strapped it onto his right shoulder and walked the sidewalk to the end of the block, then crossed Bank Street in the crosswalk. He advanced west, nearing a doctor's office. He moved his vision about; nobody seemed to be looking his way so without ceasing any footsteps, he let the colorful backpack slide down his arm, causing it to land next to the door of the doctor's office. He continued to the end of the block, crossed again over Bank Street, making a complete circle back to his truck.

As he drove away, he glanced at the lone backpack, then turned the corner onto Sixth Street. "I hope my plan works."

Dominique and Ian were weary when they arrived home and entered in through the anterior door of the house. Ian wore dry chocolate on his face as well as his shirt.

"We stopped at the Tall Pine for an ice cream cone," Ian told Travis who was sitting on the love seat.

"I can tell."

Dominique stepped to and sat upon the arm of the couch next to Matt. "I drove around on all the back roads in Pinehurst looking in back yards or alleys to see if I could spot Nathan anywhere."

He wrapped his arm around her waist. "No luck huh?"

She gently shook her head no. "I also pinned a few fliers around town."

Adam and Rainy listened with concern, then offered their help in the search.

"I'll take you up on that sometime," Dominique remarked.

CHAPTER EIGHT

Creeping Dangerously

The telephone rang. Dominique jumped out of bed and hastened to answer it. "Hello?"

"Dominique—This is Detective Morris. We found something that may have belonged to Nathan."

"May have?" she questioned with fear.

"Can you come to Wallace and identify it?"

"I'll be there after I take a shower." She set the receiver down and rushed back to her bedroom. She quickly told Matt where she was planning to depart to, then as she stepped into the master bathroom, she tore her pajamas from her warm body.

Nathan lifted and heaved a fifty pound rock into the wheelbarrow. He repeated his lift with a second boulder and let it drop next to the first one, then he pushed the metal cart to the edge of the back yard. He paused with a heavy sigh before taking hold of a rock and raising it to the rim of the wooden fence. He mounted it to the top, pushed it over and heard as it landed with a thud.

As he stepped backwards, his stomach grumbled. "Ohh . . ." he moaned to himself, "I need some food." But he knew it was scarce—at least for him. He began to think about his mom and his home—wanting to be there.

He stepped to the wheelbarrow and hoisted the second rock up and over the fence. He brushed the dirt from his hands and while he pushed the empty one-wheeled vehicle back to the middle of the yard, he caught sight of Luke climbing up onto the roof of the house. "How's he doing that?" he whispered as he advanced slightly to his left for a peek. He spotted a trellis.

While he loaded a few more boulders into the wheelbarrow, he observed Luke sitting upon the shingles near the ridgeboard, talking on his cell phone.

Dominique and Matt arrived into Wallace, parked their truck alongside the curb, and entered into the Public Safety Building. They walked up to the counter and was soon escorted back to Detective Morris' office.

Detective Morris greeted and invited them to have a seat. He could see the interest and want in Dominique's eyes. "Someone brought this in." He lifted an orange backpack from beside his desk and set it in her view. "They found it down the street from here, by Doctor Roberts office."

Her eyes widened. She felt a nauseous sensation in the pit of her stomach as she leaned forward to take hold and observe the bag. "It looks like his."

"His name is written on the inside," the detective stated.

She unzipped and looked in the backpack to see that it was empty. "I never wrote his name in here, he must of done it."

Detective Morris withdrew a large paper bag from his desk drawer and opened it up. He took the backpack from Dominique and inserted it into the paper bag. "I'm sending this to the lab. They'll be able to find any foreign hairs, fibers, or maybe a fingerprint."

Dominique's thoughts were rapid. "So how is that going to help find Nathan?"

"It may not help find him right away. If they can extract some DNA or a print from it, we could match it up to whoever took him."

"How long is this going to take?"

"It can take up to four weeks."

Her throat went dry.

"What we are going to do now is call in volunteers from the community as well as every available law enforcement officer and search and rescue teams to help find him."

"It's about time they put together a search instead of thinking one of us hurt him," she told Matt as they walked outside to their vehicle.

He lit a cigarette. "Does Nathan even know anybody in Wallace?"

"I don't think so. They found the backpack here in Wallace so I guess that's why they've decided to start their search here."

"Dominique—I want you to prepare yourself . . ." He cast his eyes her way before starting the engine. "They'll be looking for his body."

"No!" she responded quickly, "I'm not going to think that way." She turned her head and looked out the passenger window. "I think someone took him."

"I sure hope you're right."

Nathan was tired and achy from a day of moving heavy rocks. After a cool shower, he ingested three soft tacos and some Spanish rice to settle his grumbles. He soon joined Luke and Reddy in the living room for an evening of movies and smoking weed. He sat beside Critter and enjoyed holding her hand and touching her bare leg when her brothers weren't looking.

When the second movie came to an end, many yawns went around the room. Critter was the first to say good night and go to bed. After Reddy inserted a third movie into the VCR, Nathan stretched his stiff body, then arose from the love seat with a groan. He stepped to the other side of the living room and plopped himself onto the blue couch, his bed. He closed his eyes.

The next conscious memory he had was him awaking from a deep sleep. The place was dark; Luke and Reddy had gone to bed. He sat up and pushed the glow light on his watch. "One-thirty." He yawned, then gave thought to Luke's cell phone. He recalled how he and Sandy would give each other secret missions, ordering each to sneak into their own mother's room for a cigarette and a pinch of weed or he would send Ian in to find the Christmas list. Sometimes Dominique would even be in her bed sleeping when they carried out their stints.

Nathan stood to his bare feet. Yet after two hours of sleep, he still felt achy. He stepped silently through the dark living room and into the dark kitchen. As he neared the hallway, he could see the outline of Luke's bedroom door because of the night-light emitting from the bathroom. He stopped at the outside of the bathroom and shut the door quietly.

While he stood idle in pure darkness, he faced Luke and Reddy's closed bedroom door, trying to convince and prepare himself for entering. The butterflies were flapping violently inside his stomach and his palms were becoming sweaty. As he stepped to the door and placed his grip onto the knob, his heart beat fast. Because of sudden fear, he let loose of the knob. He inhaled a deep breath, let it out, then went down on his knees. "Don't get caught Nathan," he whispered to himself. He reached up and again grabbed the knob. This time he turned it. He slowly inched the door open, hoping for no squeaks or creaks.

When the door was open far enough for him to enter, he slowly crawled in. As he approached the stern of the bunk bed, one of the twins moved in his sleep. He froze and while he waited to make sure they remained sleeping, he concentrated on his breathing, trying to keep it quiet.

He continued creeping dangerously toward the night table where he had seen Luke place his phone once before. He lifted his arm and gently felt for the device, being careful to not touch any buttons when he found it nor to let his fingers rattle some loose change.

After two minutes of painstakingly searching, Nathan still on his knees, was on his way out of the bedroom with his find. Midway through the room, one of the brothers blew a loud fart. He had to quickly press his hand onto his mouth so he wouldn't laugh.

He was soon closing his kidnappers bedroom door. He wore a large smile as he tiptoed to the bathroom and opened its door before backtracking through the dark kitchen to the darken living room where he sat on the edge of his couch bed. "I'm going home!" He bent down and groped for his shoes.

Nathan unfastened the anterior door of the house and stepped outside to blackness. The quarter moon was faint and there were no street or city lights to help guide his way; he had to go on memory.

After stumbling over a rock and falling to his knees, he soon came to the side of the house where he had earlier spied Luke climbing the trellis. He gazed upward and saw nothing but the stars. As he held the phone with a firm grip, he ascended the wooden structure and advanced onto the skirt of the roof. He crawled the slope to the ridgeboard and sat. He then moved the wireless gadget into his view and lifted the cover.

When the light came on, he noticed the low battery signal. "Oh no!" he groaned. He dialed his home telephone number and fixed the cell phone to his ear. It was ringing.

Adam yawned. He and Matt had been drinking and talking the past few hours, mainly of the Underdog's bounty experiences. Everyone else had gone to bed; the doors were locked and only the radiance from the television lighted the room.

"I can't believe you two stopped in Las Vegas and got married," Matt spoke with congratulations in his voice.

"I can't believe it either," Adam replied, "With the baby on the way, we thought it would be best. Rainybow was afraid to say anything; she wanted to keep quiet about it til we got settled, but now she's starting to show."

Matt thought, trying to picture her posture. "Yea, I guess she is looking a little plump in the gut." He took a drag from his cigarette. "So are you wanting a boy or a girl?"

"Oh, it's a boy. The doctor told us that before we left and Rainy has already named him. She wants to call him Joshy."

The telephone rang. "Who in the world?" Matt questioned as he glanced at the device. When he arose for the couch, it rang again. He staggered toward and lifted the receiver. "Hello?"

Nathan heard Matt's greeting, then the connection went dead. "Matt? Matt?" he called in desperation, then he quickly took the phone away from his ear to redial. Nothing happened; the batteries held no more energy. "No . . . I want to go home." He almost cried.

After sitting on the rooftop in the dark for nearly a half an hour, he decided to dismount and return to his bed, but first he had to put Luke's cell phone back or at least set it somewhere to make him think he left it there.

In the days to come, he would have to keep an eye out for the charger, then repeat his nighttime creeping.

Matt downed three pain relievers with a gulp of cola, then he burped.

"Good morning," Dominique greeted as she entered the kitchen. "Or should I say good afternoon?"

He tried to smile at her.

"You look sick?"

He nodded.

She knew it was a hangover so she giggled within herself.

He lit a cigarette and coughed as he stepped to the unclosed back door. "There was a phone call last night."

"Yea?" She advanced toward him.

"After I answered it, the line went dead."

"It was Nathan!" she quickly remarked, "The kidnappers caught him trying to call." She paused, changing the tone of her voice to worry. "I hope they didn't hurt him."

"You don't know for sure if it was him. Don't get yourself all worked up over it."

She stepped to the counter, lit a cigarette, and thought more of the phone call, wishing she had answered the call herself. "I'm gonna have a phone installed by my side of the bed."

CHAPTER NINE

A Community Search

Ian slithered out of his bedroom and tiptoed with caution through the living room carrying Nathan's BB gun. He went to the threshold of the kitchen where he spied on his mom with the pop of his head around the frame. She had her hands to her face and he knew she was wiping a tear, but the ten year old boy wanted to play so he jumped into her view and pointed the rifle. "Freeze lady!"

She turned and looked at him with a frown.

"It's not loaded," he defended as he drew it downward.

"But you know not to point it at people—Don't let Matt see you doing it," she warned.

"Are you crying for Nathan again?"

"Yea." She stepped to and gave him a hug.

Ian left the kitchen and went scouting for other potential victims to scare or annoy. He went up the staircase to seek Travis, only he wasn't there so he stepped further down the hall to Nathan's bedroom. As he cast his eyes about the room, he wished he could shoot the mini steel balls at his brother, except he knew if Nathan were here, he would be the one to give chase, take his gun back, and shoot him.

He returned to the main floor of the house and roamed the area. He came upon the sounds of a video game being played from his mom's bedroom. He stopped at the edge of the door and peeked into the room.

He saw Matt sitting on his chair with a wireless controller in his hands. The television screen displayed a warrior trying to slay two dragons with a golden lance.

As Ian walked past the open door, he looked in, setting his vision onto his inattentive step dad. He turned himself around and walked past the door again exhibiting the BB gun. With a third pass by the open doorway, he pulled the trigger, making a click sound. He stood beside the wall, listening. He heard Matt pressing buttons on his controller so he boldly stepped in the doorway holding the rifle in front of him. He glared at Matt, then pulled the trigger so the gun would click again.

"You're not suppose to play with that in the house," Matt warned.

He stood idle with a smirk on his face and clicked it a third time.

"Don't stand there and stare at me!"

Ian snickered to himself.

Matt pushed pause and when he arose, Ian scampered away. He closed the door.

There was a hard knock at the entrance door of the house. Travis quit eyeballing his new tattoo in front of the full-length mirror and left the laundry room to go answer it.

"Swade needs us today," William Hoffman spoke to Travis and Matt as he entered in.

"Oh boy," Matt remarked as he rubbed his chin. "I'm suppose to help in the community search for Nathan today."

"I understand your prior commitment, but Swade is going to be out fifteen grand if we don't go get this fugitive."

Matt sighed. "Let me go tell my wife."

Without wanting to be too obvious, Travis emphasized his intention of rounding up the newest and only rookie of their hire.

"Maybe the newest," William agreed in jest, "but not the only greenhorn . . ."

Some five minutes later, Adam left with his fellow mentors to discuss the details of their bounty at the Underdog's office.

Dominique dropped Ian off with his Grandma Ilene in Pinehurst, a rarity, and headed to Wallace with Nick and Rainy as her passengers to aid in the search for her third born. When they arrived into the small town, there were scads of people and nowhere to park.

"We're going to be doing a lot of walking," Nick remarked.

"Are you sure you're up to it?" Dominique turned herself to an expectant Rainy and asked.

"I could always rest, sit on a big rock or log," she replied.

"We won't stay long. The volunteers could do all the trampling on the dirt roads in the woods. We'll go up by Nine Mile Road."

After finding a spot to park her car, Dominique cut the engine. She took a deep breath and held onto the steering wheel with a firm grip. The more she thought about it, the more she really didn't want to be there. She didn't know if she should help in the search; she didn't want to be the one to find her son's body. She didn't think she would be able to handle a thing like that. She felt herself begin to shake so she said a quick prayer and lit a cigarette.

"Are you okay Mom?"

"Sort-of." She told them how she was feeling, then decided she would just go try to locate Detective Morris to see if he had anything to say.

While the bounty hunters geared up, William wrote the details of their days' purpose on the marker board.

"Her name is Kimberly Brothers. She has a number of aliases. She's five foot ten."

"She's taller than you Travis," Adam poked.

"I'll still take her down. I don't pump these bad boys for nothing," he boasted of his biceps as he flexed them.

"She weighs one hundred and fifty pounds—she may be able to run fast boys. It says here that she's a coach for a soccer team."

"We'll wear our sneakers."

William continued. "She's charged with two counts of credit card fraud. She knows she's done wrong." He paused. "When I talked to Swade earlier, he had said Kim's sister, the co-signer, didn't want to lose her car so she's willing to help." He stepped to his desk, picked up three photo copies of Kim's picture, and gave one to each agent to look over while he prepared to make a phone call.

Matt, Travis, and Adam took in the features of her round head that was colored with long black hair and brown eyes.

"She looks like my wife," Adam commented, "but my Rainybow is prettier."

"Oh . . . you poor lovesick puppy," Travis expressed in a low tone.

"Hey—At least I have a woman."

"I have a girlfriend," he defended, "I just haven't brought her home to meet my mom yet."

"Oh . . . she's that kind of girlfriend."

William set the receiver to the base and looked at his partner. "No one is answering. We'll have to drive over there."

Dominique, Nick, and Rainy approached a gathering of people who were wearing sheriff and rescue uniforms. She scanned the faces of the law enforcement and before she could locate the detective, a reporter from channel one came up to her. "Are you Nathan's mother?"

She nodded.

"I thought so." The reporter turned and signaled for her cameraman to turn on the camera and roll tape. "Dominique—How hopeful are you that some evidence will be found here today?" She moved the microphone close to Dominique's mouth.

"Not hopeful at all," she replied, "I still have hope that he's alive somewhere."

"Why do you think that? Or do you have any proof he's alive?"

"No proof, just a gut feeling."

"People can't just go on gut feelings."

Dominique frowned at the reporter. "I can and I will."

"Good for you then," she replied, "Do you have anything you want to say to the alleged kidnappers?"

She faced the camera and told herself to speak boldly. "I want to ask the person or persons who took my son to please release him." She felt her voice quivering, but she continued on. "Nathan is a child of the Most High God and if you hurt him, God will surely get you!" She cast her eyes onto the reporter. "Please excuse me now." She stepped away to join her oldest son and niece while the newscaster ended her report into the camera.

The four bounty hunters traveled to and arrived at an apartment complex on the southeast side of Coeur d' Alene. They scanned the area and kept an eye out for Kimberly and her blue sedan as they approached and knocked on a door. After a few moments, the structure opened.

"Hi Ella?" William spoke up, exposing his badge, and asked if Kim was around while Matt stayed back four feet beside the exterior wall and Travis and Adam positioned themselves one on each end of the building.

Ella knew they were the men Swade sent over. "No, she's not here right now. She was here two days ago with Eddie."

"Her boyfriend?"

"Yes," she confirmed. "After Swade called me this morning, I kept trying to call her, but she wouldn't answer her cell phone."

"Can you give me her number? Just in case it's a different number than what's in her file."

"Yea, come on in."

William radioed to Travis and Adam his action report while he and Matt stepped into Ella's apartment in a watchful manner.

"To make matters worse, my checkbook is missing. I only had two checks left in that booklet, but to have my own sister steal them is pretty hurtful."

"How do you know she stole them?" Matt questioned.

"A clerk from the Corner Gas Station called me. He knew something funny was going on so I went down there and paid cash for Kim's purchase and he was nice enough to give the check back to me."

"Can I see that check?"

After William and Matt inspected the letter of credit, they left Ella's residence with Kimberly's cell phone number and the name of the gas station clerk.

"Let's stay on her trail," Matt encouraged to the rookies as they walked to the SUV.

Returning to and sitting in the driver's seat, William used his cell phone to dial Kimberly. With no answer, he closed his phone and drove away.

"Can you tell us what happened?" William asked the store clerk after he identified himself as a bounty hunter.

"Sure. Ella or should I say Kim?" He moved his fingers as to make bunny ears. "Kim tried to buy a carton of cigarettes and while I was processing the check, her male companion took the cigarettes outside. She told me she left her identification in the car, she went to go get it and never returned. I decided then to call the phone number on the check."

"Why didn't you call the police instead?"

"I recognized the address on the check. She's my neighbor."

"You're just a good Samaritan, huh?"

"Well, you know how it goes, she's pretty . . . I didn't want to see her get into any trouble."

William smiled at him. "What time yesterday did Kim come into the store?"

"About eleven o'clock."

"We're twenty-three hours behind her," Travis commented as he eyed his watch.

They stepped outside to their vehicle. "I wish I knew where this punk Eddie lived," William remarked, then his cell phone rang.

"She just called me," Swade told him.

"Kim?"

"Yea, she knows we're looking for her."

"How in the hell would she know so quickly?"

"I don't know, but she told me she had some things to take care of before she meets with us."

"Not today. She ain't going to waste my time!" William vented.

Matt, Travis, and Adam listened in while William wrote Kim's new number on his note pad.

"How many numbers does this girl have?" Matt whispered to the rookies.

"We'll get her!" William told the bail bondsman, then ended the call. He turned to his partner. "You want to handle this one?"

"Not really," Matt responded, "Travis is better at communicating than I am."

William breathed in and exhaled heavily. Frustrated that HE was doing almost everything, he handed the piece of paper with the phone number to Travis.

Travis withdrew his own wireless phone from his pocket and after they climbed into the Explorer for privacy, he dialed the number.

"Hello?" a woman answered.

"Where are you Kim?" Travis scolded while the crew raised their eyebrows with interest.

"Who wants to know?" the inebriated woman slurred.

"I'm a bounty hunter for Swade from Quest Bail Bonds, remember him?"

"Of course I remember him. I'm not stupid."

"Why didn't you remember to go to court then?"

She was quiet. "Are you cute?"

"Huh?" He was stumped, but quickly shook it off. "Where are you? We need to meet up and get this paperwork taken care of, then you can be on your way," he fabricated.

With of push of a button, she ended the call.

Travis pulled the phone away from his ear. "She hung up."

"Call her back!"

"Hold on!" He bowed his head and closed his eyes as he commenced to heavy thought. "I heard something in the background . . . A bell. I've heard this bell before."

"Whad it sound like?"

He thought that to be an odd question. "Ding-dong, ding-dong, like a church bell."

"Could it be the Morning Glory Church bell over on Bayview Avenue?" Matt submitted with urgency.

"Maybe. Let's go there."

William started the engine and drove off. While he accelerated down Fifteenth Street, Travis tried to call Kim again, but she never picked up.

"Look for her blue sedan with a white hood," Matt reminded the gang.

William traveled over the speed limit for a half a mile, but had to slow as they entered a school zone and by-passed a football field. Two more blocks and he turned west on Bayview Avenue. "We're almost there," William announced, "Keep your eyes open."

They soon came upon a huge architectural building and while they drove the anterior side, they gazed upward at the large bell in the steeple. They also scanned the parking area, but didn't see any blue sedans with a white hood. They hastened to the rear parking lot and searched from their open windows.

"I'll be damned! There's a blue sedan," Travis said to his co-workers.

William stopped his vehicle to let them out, then he quickly found a space to park while the three crept to the desired vehicle.

Upon arrival, they peeked with caution through the windows and saw that it was vacant of Kim or her boyfriend. However, the car was full of empty beer cans that were strewn about.

"This is her car," Matt verified after casting his eyes onto the license plate. "She's gotta be in that church." He directed the two rookies with a point of his finger toward the huge building, then radioed to William of their intentions.

William remained by the blue sedan while the team rushed toward the church entrance. After they arrived at the solid double doors, Matt reached out and pressed down on the metal latch to open the door, then he pushed the structure forward so they could enter.

As they set foot into the foyer, they saw Kim sitting on a chair, talking to the priest. They advanced toward her.

She looked up at them and noticed their black clothes and badges before speaking. "You can't take me, I'm pleading sanctuary!"

"You can't plead sanctuary," Matt deemed, "We're not in ancient Rome."

She positioned her fists in front of her. "You'll have to get by these then cuz I'm not leaving this church."

The priest arose from his chair and stepped back.

Matt glanced at Travis and Adam with a cracked smile, then focused in on her. "We can spray you with pepper spray if need be."

"Go ahead," she yelled, "Then I'll sue!"

The three men lunged for Kim, each trying to grab a limb. She began swinging and kicking. Matt had a hold of one arm, but her other arm was still loose; her fist connected to Adam's eye.

She continued to fight. Adam withdrew from the ruckus, being temporarily fazed. "That bitch can hit."

Matt took hold of his pepper can and sprayed a small amount in her face, then Travis yanked her from her seat and forced her to the floor.

She was screaming and pleading sanctuary while she continued to wrestle them.

Travis and Matt together restrained her with their weight and soon had her handcuffed. They all were panting for air and Matt radioed to William to bring water.

"Another payday for us!" Travis boasted as he arose to his feet.

Dominique, Nick, and Rainy were perched on a log, taking a cigarette break. They had just walked a mile up Nine Mile Road and a mile back.

"I'm thirsty."

"Yea, me too," Dominique agreed. "We can walk to the cafe and get us some Cokes or water."

The nearby expanse where everyone was once gathered was now bare of volunteers on account they had been dispatched to the back roads and surrounding rough and overgrown hills. There was a breeze to help the trio keep cool as the sun provided its heat on that bright day.

Dominique, Nick, and Rainy walked the long block and soon arrived at the small eatery. They purchased their drinks and were sitting on a bench outside the building when four people rushed by on the sidewalk.

"They found some bones!" one woman announced to her confidants.

"Oh my God!" Dominique blurted out in horror as she arose to her feet and watched them hasten down the street. She turned and cast her eyes to Nick. "I can't . . ." Her throat went dry as she tried to speak. "I can't handle this."

Nick arose to his feet and stood beside her. Concern was emitting from his face.

Dominique touched her hand to her chest. "I can't breathe very well." She felt her palms becoming sweaty, then she collapsed onto the bench.

"Mom?" He sat next to her. "Are you going to be okay?"

Rainy listened in and beheld the situation.

Dominique's complexion was pale. "Nathan? Oh my Nathan. What happened to you? What did you go through?" Tears streamed down her cheeks as she thought about those bones.

"Do you want me to follow those people?" Nick asked.

Rainy perked up. "You can't leave me alone with her!" she demanded in a fearful manner.

Dominique was unmindful of what her oldest son was asking. She gazed forward as if in a trance, still pressing her hand onto her throbbing chest.

"Do you want to go to the hospital?"

She didn't answer.

Nick looked at Rainy. "Maybe she's praying."

"The hospital is a good idea," Rainy urged.

After acquiring the keys, he hurried to fetch the car.

Dominique forced a breath of air into her lungs, then exhaled. "I'm scared."

Rainy didn't know what to say.

Upon arrival at the hospital, the nurse took an overwrought Dominique back to the emergency room where she had her lay on an examination bed. She spoke of her symptoms and that she thought it was a respiratory or cardiac problem, but she didn't talk of what caused her to respond in that way.

The nurse asked some routine questions, then checked the patient's pulse and temperature before the doctor entered into the room.

The doctor ordered a blood sample to be taken to check her iron level. As the needle was injected, she grew woozy. Her legs became restless and she began to sweat.

Soon after, the doctor prescribed medication to relax her, then ordered her to be hooked up to the heart monitor. As she lay there, the machine beeping, her mind was focused in on her missing and perhaps dead son.

Nick and Rainy were in the waiting room when Nick decided to call Detective Morris.

"I'll go with you," Rainy suggested.

He first searched the hospital for a phone book, then used his cell phone to call the sheriff's department where he obtained the detective's cell number.

The detective answered his portable phone after two rings.

"Hi Detective Morris? This is Nick, Dominique Jax's son."

"Hi Nick, how can I help you?"

"We overheard someone saying that some bones were found up in the canyon today. Can you tell me about that?"

"Yea, they found some bones, but they turned out to be deer bones."

CHAPTER TEN

Liar, Liar

"None of your business!" the cranky woman told her overbearing landlord as she stood by her open front door.

"It is my business," he yelled, "You're living in my building!"

Luke stepped into the living room and glanced at the television, then at Critter. "What are you watching?"

"My soap," she replied, "This lady is about to get evicted from her apartment."

While she continued to surrender to her show, Luke headed out to the back yard to hang with and observe the progress of his brother's work. All the large rocks had been removed, the trees were trimmed, and a sizable pile of branches lay in the center of the yard, waiting to be burnt.

"Time to take a break," Reddy called out to Nathan as he walked toward the porch.

With a red, sweaty face, Nathan joined him. He sat on a lawn chair and wiped his brow before taking a drink of his warm lemonade. "Yuck!" He looked at Reddy. "Isn't it your turn to get the ice cubes?"

"You get the refills again and I'll grab a joint."

"Sounds good."

Soon enough, Nathan was slumbering in his chair, high on THC. He thought about how hot of a day it is and how nice it would be to go swimming or tubing down the river with his family—he was missing his home again.

Luke eyed the pile of cut branches. "Did you get the permit to burn?"

"Pa got it and gave it to me before he left."

Nathan raked some weeds and dead leaves toward the pile of branches and heaved them atop, trying to build a gigantic mass. Maybe, he thought, if he erected it high enough, the fire marshal will see the smoke and come out, then he could go home without any trouble.

"He's bouncing that ball in the house again!" Matt grumbled to Dominique upon arriving into the kitchen. "He knows it makes me mad."

"Is he doing it near you?"

"Does it matter?" he snapped.

"Yes it does." She gave him a look of disapproval. "He's allowed to play wall-ball in his bedroom. I've told you that."

"Balls are made for outside!"

"Says your mean father!"

He turned and stomped off.

"You have a callous heart!" she yelled, thinking and realizing she may have made a mistake marrying him. Although she loved him, she was beginning to see a side of him she didn't like.

A while later, Matt returned to the kitchen and told his wife he was leaving to go put gas in his truck.

"I'll see you in a bit then? I'm gonna start dinner soon."

"Yea," he answered.

During the next hour, Dominique baked, fried, and boiled. She was filling the sink with dishwater when she heard the rear door of the house open. "Matt?"

"No—it's me."

She recognized the voice. "Hi Nick."

"Mm . . . I smell fried chicken and buns."

"You're just in time if you want to stay and eat."

Ian entered the kitchen. "I washed my hands. Is dinner ready?"

"Have a seat. I guess we'll start without Matt." She looked at Nick. "You didn't see him outside, did you?"

"No—his truck is gone."

"He went to go get gas an hour ago," she told her son.

"Hmm?"

"Yea, he was kind of upset when he left. Ian was playing wall-ball in his room." Her facial expression represented scorn.

Nick shook his head in amazement as he piled mashed potatoes onto his plate.

"Matt's a big crybaby," Ian added.

"Keep that comment to yourself," Dominique told him. "Most of the time you try to annoy him."

"It's fun."

"It's disrespectful."

The fire roared. Nathan used the hose to spray water onto the outskirts of the large flame. Standing near the blaze made it an even hotter late June day for him so he periodically splashed water to his face and bare chest.

After there was enough water on the ground, he stepped back and as he moved to go turn off the water, he noticed Critter standing on the porch. She wore a gaze and a thin white sundress. He could see the shape of her tiny hips and thighs through the outfit. He quickly spied on Luke and Reddy to see if they were watching him, then he advanced to the spout. When he returned, Critter was still standing in the same spot.

Reddy approached him with a warning. "I saw you looking at my sister. Don't be looking at her that way."

"Can I help it what she wears?"

He didn't reply, but rather stepped to the porch and offered his advice to Critter to go change her clothes.

"I can wear what I want!" she expressed with resistance.

"Not with strange boys around."

"He's not strange."

Reddy thought for a moment. "If you want him to keep looking, I can rip your dress off for you and that'll give him a real good peek," he spoke in a threatening way.

"You're a jerk!" She spun around and stomped into the house.

After a cool shower, Nathan went to the front porch. He was still hoping someone, a forest ranger or a fire chief, would arrive for an observation and he wanted to be ready if they did.

Critter who was now dressed in jean shorts and a tank top, stepped out onto the porch. "You wanna come inside and watch a movie?" she asked him.

"No—I just want to sit out here for a while."

She joined him on the wooden bench.

"Have you had any trouble with wild animals up here?"

"You mean like bears or mountain lions?"

"Yea."

"Not lately."

He was quiet for a moment then cast his vision upon her. "If I were to walk to Pinehurst, how long do you think it would take me?"

"Why would you walk that far?" she questioned.

"I wanna go home."

Luke overheard from the open doorway. "You want to go home?" he taunted as he stepped forward.

Nathan spun his attention his way.

"Here then." He tossed his cell phone to him. "Call someone."

Nathan knew or at least he thought he knew that the phone was still dead, but he tried to dial out anyways.

Luke broke out in laughter.

Nathan's face became red. He set the portable phone onto the bench and stood to his feet. "I demand that you take me home!" He glared at Luke, then at Reddy who was now standing beside his brother.

"Don't you like us anymore?" Luke teased.

"That's not the point," he yelled, "You told me on the second day I was here that you'd take me home!"

"Things change."

He felt his insides boil. He wanted to slug him.

"You look angry?"

Nathan turned away from them, jumped the two steps to the ground, and walked past their truck to the end of the gravel driveway.

"Where are you going?" Reddy called out when Nathan reached the scanty dirt lane.

"I'm going home!"

The twins looked at each other.

"You can't let my boyfriend go!" Critter exclaimed to her brothers as she arose from the bench.

Luke and Reddy jumped the steps as well and rushed after their escapee.

"Leave me alone!" Nathan commanded as they approached him.

"You need to stop now and come back."

"Why?" He paused his walking and cast another glare their way. "Why can't I just go home?"

"We don't want you to."

"I don't care." He took off walking again.

They went after him. When Reddy reached out and grabbed Nathan's arm, Nathan pulled it back, twisting himself around. He then swung his other arm, aiming his fist toward Reddy's face, but missed.

"Oh-ho . . . You didn't just swing at me?" Reddy stepped forward and pushed Nathan, using his foot to trip him.

Luke stood and watched.

Nathan who was lying on the ground, retaliated by kicking back, then he quickly rolled over and arose to his feet. He presented his fists, ready for a battle.

Luke laughed.

Reddy brought his fists up to chest level and eyed the scrapper. "You want to fight me?"

"Not really," Nathan replied, "I just want to go home."

Critter came running. "Don't fight!" she yelled as she stepped in between them, facing Nathan. "Don't go home," she pleaded, "I love you." She placed her hand over her mouth, she had let her feelings loose.

Nathan lowered his fists. He could see the sincerity and embarrassment in her face. He didn't want to bleed from being hit nor did he want to feel any pain so he figured he would prepare himself for the journey and set out for home another time.

The dishes were done. A man's serving of fried chicken, mashed potatoes, and dinner rolls lay wrapped on a plate, set atop of the microwave.

Dominique and Nick sat on the back porch swing and enjoyed a joint while Ian lay on the trampoline, moaning over a too full of a tummy.

"No more community searches for me," Dominique told her son, "After that panic attack, I'll just let the authorities and volunteers handle it."

"You're not giving up, are you?"

"No. I'll never give up on Nathan."

The back door opened and the newlyweds exited the house. They joined Dominique and Nick on the partially isolated porch.

"Hey!" Rainy greeted, "Look what I bought for Joshy in town today." She held up an infant's baseball pajamas.

"That is really cute," Dominique replied.

Adam scanned the area. "So . . . where's Uncle Matt?" he questioned.

"I'm not for sure," she answered, then disclosed why.

The sun had left the western sky for the day when Matt staggered in through the front door. Dominique couldn't believe her eyes as she watched him continue on toward their bedroom. "Where was the gas station?" she asked him with sarcasm, "In Canada?"

"I didn't go to Canada," he slurred.

"Obviously," she replied, smelling the liquor. She followed him into their bedroom. "Why do you treat me this way?"

"What way?" He flopped his rear onto to edge of the bed almost bouncing to the floor.

"You don't even see it, do you?"

He was silent.

"You told me you were going to go get gas. I said 'see you in a bit' and you return six hours later, drunk off your ass?"

"I did get gas."

Nick was standing in the open doorway, wanting to say good bye to his mother so he could head home. Dominique saw him and left the room.

"It's useless Mom," he told her as they stepped into the hall.

She knew he was right.

"Why do you put up with his crap? He's nothing but a liar."

"I don't know. He's not a bad guy when he's sober or stoned."

"Only to you. He's always giving glares to us boys."

"I'm sorry he does that."

They heard a loud thud. Dominique rushed into and through her bedroom to the bathroom where she saw Matt positioned face down on the floor between the toilet and bathtub. His pants were down. She wanted to laugh at his state of blunder as she watched him push himself up to his knees, then she asked, "Are you okay?"

"No," he groaned.

"What's wrong?" She leaned in and peeked to see if there was any blood. After seeing none and receiving no answer from him, she slipped away to the living room where she slept for the night.

CHAPTER ELEVEN

Boobs

Matt was examining his arm, barely touching it when he stepped into Dominique's office. She seemed to be writing at her desk, heavy in thought. "I think I need to go see a doctor."

She broke her daze and looked up at him. "Why—did you hurt yourself?" she smirked, recalling his fall from the night before.

"My elbow hurts. It's swollen."

"What happened?" She wanted to see if he remembered.

"I don't know."

"Do you remember coming home last night?"

"Sure I do."

Matt left the clinic with his arm in a sling. He had Dominique drive him to the pharmacy for his pain pills, then to the Underdog's office.

When he entered into the suite, William was standing at his desk, lifting a navy blue t-shirt out from a postal box.

William cast his eyes upon him. "What happened to you? Chasing criminals without me?"

He grinned. "I fell." He stepped in close to him and observed the new company shirts that sported their logo.

"There's two for each of us." He was silent as he withdrew the rest of the shirts from the box.

"This hurt arm is why I stopped by, to let you know I'll be somewhat out of commission for a week or two."

"One less man to help take down the bail jumpers," he responded with dismay. "You don't haggle, you don't do paperwork. What are you going to do for the company-" He raised his hands and demonstrated bunny ears as he finished speaking. "while you're out of commission?"

"I'm your financial partner. That's enough until I heal."

"You got me there Pal." He cast a smile his way. "We're dead for a couple days anyways."

It was the end of the week. Adam had completed his thirty-two hour training course and was awaiting for next Friday to arrive so he could take his written exam. He was feeling pumped, aching to go catch a bounty when William called the house with a case.

"The chase is on!" Adam exclaimed as he threw his new t-shirt on, then geared up. He kissed his pregnant wife good bye and left with Travis and Matt for the office.

"I'm sorry," Critter spoke to Nathan as she sat down on the couch next to him. "I'm sorry you're so miserable."

"If you were really sorry, you'd help me go home." He continued playing his video game without looking aside at her.

"Maybe soon I can help you if . . ." She stopped, unsure if she should even ask.

"If what?"

"If you help me run away to my grandmother's house."

"Where does she live?"

"Oregon."

"Oregon?" He paused his game and turned his eyes to the two doorways to make sure Luke was still in his bedroom, then looked at her. "Where in Oregon?"

"Rainier."

He thought. "Isn't that on the coast?"

"Almost."

"Damn Woman!" he replied, "That's a way's away. Why would you want to go all the way to her house?"

"I love my grandma."

They heard a vehicle advance and park in the driveway outside. "Reddy's home," Critter spoke as she arose and stepped to the door. She turned and gestured with her finger to her lips for Nathan to not speak about their conversation, then opened the door.

Reddy neared, carrying two gallons of milk. "There's more in the truck."

Nathan stood to his feet to go offer his assistance.

"Wait until you smell what I got," Reddy told Nathan when they crossed paths.

"Billy Boobs Peterson is his name . . ." Swade, the bail bondsman began to say.

"Boobs?" Travis interrupted with a smile.

"Yea. His nickname is Boobs cuz he has boobs."

Everyone chuckled.

"Don't chuckle too long boys. He's a six foot two, three hundred pound man."

"Damn!" Adam exclaimed.

"Still feeling eager?" Matt asked him.

"We're going to get our asses kicked."

"Let's focus now," William edged in, then read from Billy's rap sheet. "He's got a whole list of stuff, the most recent being illegal discharge of a firearm, possession of drugs and drug paraphernalia." He lifted and cast his eyes about the employees. "Swade will lose a lot of money if Boob's isn't found and brought in."

Travis and Adam laughed.

"Billy. We'll call him Billy among us," he spoke in humor, "since Boobs is too funny for everyone. Also, I've called in Nick because Matt is unusable."

Within the minute, Nick arrived. He threw on a company t-shirt while William passed out Billy's mugshot to each agent.

Swade spoke up. "Billy is a dangerous criminal who should never of been bonded out."

"We'll get him," William assured the bail bondsman. He looked to the rookies. "Billy's not answering his cell phone so let's start with his girlfriend since that's where he told Swade he was living." He flipped through a few pages into Billy's file. "Her name is Lisa. Swade, Matt, and Adam in one vehicle, Travis and Nick come with me."

They verified her address between them, then left the office. They drove to Post Falls, into a mobile home park, and cruised slowly upon the road and over the speed bumps.

"Space fourteen," William spoke into the portable radio to Matt's team who was traveling the horseshoe road on the opposite end of the trailer park. "Stop two or three trailers before you get to her place."

Drizzle was in the air when all but Matt stepped out of the vehicles. Nick and Adam made their way through the neighbor's yard and jumped a small fence, then went around a trailer. Nick positioned himself at the edge of the property and Adam guarded the rear door.

Swade, William, and Travis approached the main entry. Swade stood some three feet away and after confirming that everyone was in place, William knocked. With no reply, he knocked louder. "Billy—open up!"

The door opened slowly and stopped when the chain reached its bound.

"Lisa?" William asked in his bass tone.

"Yea?" she answered softly.

"I'm lookin' for Billy?" He showed his badge.

"He's not here. We broke up."

"Sure you did," William replied, "Can we come in and search?" He tried to peek within the gap.

"No." She closed the door.

"If I find out you're protecting him," he vented his threat through the wooden structure, "you're going to jail!" Frustrated, he turned and as he stepped away, he radioed for the crew to return to the vehicles.

"I think she's lying," Travis mentioned to William, "I saw a suitcase."

"Good eye, good eye Travis."

Before the bounty hunters arrived at the trucks, Nick noticed across the street, a neighbor was pruning a bush in his yard. With William accompanying him, he took a photo of Billy over to him.

"Yea, I saw him yesterday," the fellow replied after seeing the photo. "He was sitting on the trunk of that car," he pointed, "smoking a cigarette. I remember because he looked as though he was heavy in thought."

"Did you see him leave?"

"No," he answered while he gently moved his head. "I went back inside my trailer and watched tv for the rest of the day."

"Thanks for the information," Nick remarked.

William handed the man his business card. "Call me if you see him?"

He nodded.

Nick and William rebound to a waiting crew and stood beside Matt's open window. "We'll see if she and Billy are really broken up," William spoke to the squad. "Travis saw a suitcase just inside her entryway." He cast his eyes onto his watch then upon Matt. "Why don't you, Travis, and Adam stay here and spy her place. Stay in contact and if she leaves, follow her. I have to get Swade back to his office, then check things out elsewhere." He went to his truck and sped away from the area with Swade and Nick.

After dropping the bondsman off at his office, William cruised to North Coeur d'Alene to Billy's mother's house. "Go ahead and take your gear off," he told Nick, "You can pose as a friend."

Nick turned his shirt inside out and stepped out of the vehicle. William watched from the parked SUV as his informer walked down the sidewalk and across the street, through the driveway, and up to the door where he knocked.

The framed structure opened.

"Hi—I'm looking for Boobs." He felt silly saying that.

"And who are you?" she asked.

"I'm a friend. We spent time together in jail."

"Well . . . he's not here."

Nick heard from behind the door, the sound of a gun being cocked. "Okay, I'll catch up with him later." He turned and not wanting to be shot at, hurried back to the SUV. "He's in there!" Nick expressed concern.

Down the block, Travis sat in the driver's seat while Matt rode shotgun and Adam in the back seat. They were keeping watch over their target as well as the slow moving clouds and soon a yellow taxicab approached and stopped in front of Lisa's trailer. The driver honked.

All eyes were attentive.

Within the minute, Lisa advanced from her home with a suitcase and duffel bag. She let the driver stow her luggage into the trunk while she entered and sat in the cab.

"We have to follow her!" Travis thundered as he reached for and turned the key to the ignition. "Maybe that's Billy's clothes and she's going to return them to him?"

"Or she's leaving town?" Matt radioed to William of their intention while Travis accelerated, following at a near distance.

"Billy's here at his mother's house!" William announced with urgency, "Where ever Lisa is going, it won't lead you to Billy. I recommend you get over here immediately."

There was a pause over the airway.

"We're going to follow Lisa," Matt insisted, "I don't want to blow it."

"Damn it!" William tried to throw his mike, but it only hit the dashboard. "We can't do anything without back-up," he told Nick in frustration.

"Especially if he has a gun."

"If?" William turned his head and cast his eyes upon him.

"I'm pretty sure he does. I didn't see it, but I know what a gun being cocked sounds like."

William was quiet while he thought. He knew he couldn't storm into the mother's house unless . . . He withdrew his cell phone from his pocket and dialed for Swade. "What address did Billy give you on the original application form?" he asked him.

After sifting through the file, he answered West Neider Road.

"And that's where we're at now!" he replied.

"He only gave it as a mailing address. Remember he was staying with Lisa?"

"That's still good enough for me, back-up or not." He flipped his phone closed.

"That's crazy William," Nick urged, "Let's just sit here and wait it out."

Travis entered onto the freeway and sped to catch up to the yellow cab who had gained a lead because he was left behind at a red stoplight. He soon approached and drove through the Washington state line toward Spokane.

"I bet she is headin' for the airport," Matt presumed.

"We'll see where she's going first, then go assist William and Nick."

Nathan was ripped after Reddy smoked only a half a bowl of his skunk bud with both him and Luke. As he remained in a slump on the couch, the last thing he wanted to do now was yard work. He was glad when Reddy picked up a controller and challenged Luke to a game of Alienoids.

Critter set foot and stopped in the living room entry. She cast her vision onto Nathan who promptly returned the stare. She motioned with a slight lift of her head for him to follow her.

He noted that Reddy and Luke were unmindful of him as he arose and stepped through the kitchen and hallway until they arrived at her bedroom.

"What do you want?" he asked her after she sat onto her bed.

"To talk."

"I can't get caught in your bedroom, your brothers would have my nuts." Nathan stepped in and lifted the window, then climbed the ladder to her secret room.

She also scaled the parallel rungs and joined him on the floor in the center of the enclosure. "Have you thought about what I asked?"

"Not really. It's only been a half an hour, but I do have a few questions." He first leaned in and gave his girlfriend a quick kiss.

"Yea?"

"How do you suggest we get to Rainier?"

"The bus."

"Do you have any money?"

"I have about three hundred dollars saved up," she boasted with a smile.

"Damn girl!" With no other pressing questions, he cast a wishful eye at her low-cut shirt, then tilted himself toward her and whispered, "Are you wearing a bra?"

"No," she answered with a soft grin. "Do you want to see?"

"Of course." He knew from what the Bible taught that he shouldn't partake in this kind of activity, but for now he didn't care.

"Well, you are my boyfriend, so I'll let you see them."

His anticipation was great as he watched her unbutton the front, then pull her shirt apart. "Boobs! Nice boobs!" He reached forward with his hand to touch them.

CHAPTER TWELVE

Extreme Encounters

William had calmed himself by the time Matt, Travis, and Adam arrived at the scene to assist him and Nick in taking down Billy Boobs Peterson.

"Lisa got on a flight to Seattle," Matt told William and Nick.

"By herself?"

He nodded.

William wanted to say something smart, however, he thought it best to hold his tongue.

The five men stood behind their vehicles at the end of the block, finalizing their game plan and making sure they were properly suited up. Nick mentioned to the three arrivals of the loaded gun Billy carried.

"This may be our first shoot-out," William warned, "I'll take the lead, Matt's gonna sit in the truck with his hurt arm and spy from afar. If Boobs takes off running, Matt will radio his direction to us. Nick," he looked at each person as he spoke to them, "You come with me. Travis and Adam, I want you positioned at the back door."

They nodded in agreement.

William eyed the surrounding area. There was no traffic, whether by car or pedestrian. "Okay, let's go—everybody watch your head and each others back." He gave Travis and Adam a head start to their positions before he and Nick rushed up the driveway to the anterior door. He banged on the thin structure.

Nick stood with nervous energy on the opposite side of the door frame, waiting to see if the door would open. He held a container of Mace, ready to spray while William manifested a pistol.

William again leaned aside and banged on the door. "Come on out Billy, we know you're in there!"

Without warning, a shot came through the closed door, blowing a hole at midsection.

Instant dread struck Nick, but William who was more experienced and fearless, stepped in front of the door and gave a hard kick using the bottom of his boot, then quickly backed aside. "No need for gunfire Billy, just put the rifle down and come out!" They listened for movement.

Travis and Adam heard the discharge. Outfitted in their bullet proof vests, they stood beside a large tree; Travis with his pistol, ready for a gunfight.

William decided to take a peek. He popped the top portion of his head beyond he door frame and saw only the shadow of the large man as he darted into another room. "Get back here billy!" he shouted.

Billy came upon the rear exit of the house. Travis noticed that he sported no weapon as he rushed out and crossed the porch. "Freeze billy!" He aimed his pistol at him while Adam looked on.

Billy ignored the command and ran across the lawn toward an open gate.

Travis didn't want to shoot him so he fired a warning shot into the wooden fence.

The dark clouds were moving swiftly, bringing in a summer rainstorm. The gentle wind increased, making the smaller branches sway and the leaves twist and flutter.

William cautiously tailed Billy's path through the house, then gave chase once he was outside. Nick, as well as Travis and Adam, followed.

The rain poured from the sky throughout parts of Northern Idaho. It kept Nathan and his kidnappers indoors for the time being so Nathan played video games with Critter while Reddy sat at the kitchen table with Luke cleaning their rifles.

When the twins were done polishing and piecing together their firearms, Reddy stood and trained his rifle in the direction of the living room, causing Nathan to feel uneasy.

"Don't point that in the house!" Critter scolded, "You know Pa's rule."

He lowered the gun and when he neared the couch to go outside, he hissed like a cat at her.

In return, she just smiled.

From the front porch, Reddy looked through the scope to see if the sights were set as he aimed at the target on the tree. "She's ready to go!" he spoke of his rifle.

What's that suppose to mean? Nathan wondered with fear when he heard him say that.

When William and Travis exited through the open gate, Billy was gone. They hurried down the alley in the direction he was presumed to have run.

"Everybody split into two's," William ordered, then radioed to Matt requesting that he drive around the block to see if he could spot their prey.

Nick ran with William while Travis and Adam cut through a vacant lot. As they trod across the weeds and dirt, their boots began to sink into the mud. A moment later, Adam's foot gave way to the squishy goo; he slipped, going down on his butt and a hand. "Oh dang!" he roared.

Travis stopped and turned to see his colleague sitting while shaking the mud from his hand. He instantly broke out in laughter, then stepped his way to help him up. "Oh dude, William ain't gonna let you sit in his truck," he remarked as they both glanced at his soiled jeans.

Adam gave quick thought to pulling Travis into the mud for laughing at him, but knew there was no time for revengeful play. "I'll have to find a piece of plastic or something to cover the seat."

The rain was letting up. After Matt rounded the block, he saw his partner and Nick walking so he accelerated down the dead end street toward them. He drove up alongside the pair and informed them he hadn't seen Billy.

"He just disappeared!" Nick remarked, still breathing hard.

"He had to of come this way," William spoke as he turned, then walked until the pavement ceased and the terrain became gravel. As he and Nick cast their vision about the wet ground, he radioed to Travis. "Where are you two at?"

"We're coming up the alley. I can see you from here."

William whirled himself around and saw the rookies approaching.

"Here's his shoe prints, I think," Nick expressed with eagerness from some twelve feet away.

William advanced to him swiftly and looked at the muddy indents. "They're fresh."

With Nick in the lead, the three bounty hunters followed the indentations down and up a ditch toward a grove of trees. As they crossed the scanty field, the muddy ground became wet grass. William instructed Travis and Adam to enter the grove roughly ten yards away. They treaded the tiny forest, hunting for shoe prints and broken twigs or branches.

Matt had parked the truck and was using his binoculars to search the surrounding area. He soon observed a police car cruising his way. The officer pulled up behind him, then stepped out and advanced to his window.

"Hello officer," Matt greeted as he showed his badge. "Just huntin' down a bounty."

The sun was shining once again. The air was humid and hot.

"Look low," William advised to Nick. "He could be hiding in the bushes, camouflaging himself."

"Or he's already a half a mile ahead of us past these trees sneaking around the buildings, trying to blend in."

Travis and Adam were treading east through the shrubbery under the tall pine trees when they heard William yelling to Billy to climb down. They hurried his way to see what was going on. The men stood in awe as they looked upward and saw Billy siting on a limb near the top of a large tree.

"Holy crap! Who's going to climb up there and get him down?" Adam asked.

William looked at him. "You want to?"

"No."

"How are we going to get him down then?" Travis questioned.

William stepped to the base of the tree. "I'm gonna saw this mother-fuckin' tree down!" he yelled as he attempted to push and shake the trunk of it. "That's how!"

"Go ahead and saw it down, it'll be fun!" Billy yapped, "I'll yell timber." He began to break off and throw pine cones down to them, laughing when each agent stepped aside.

"He's gotta be high on something," Nick remarked as he lit a cigarette.

While he paced, William noticed Nick smoking and came up with an idea. He tilted his head upward and hollered, "You want a cigarette Billy?"

"Sure—bring one up to me."

"No, you have to come down here and get it."

"Can't do that," he shouted as he began to sway from the limb he sat on.

The onlookers watched the three hundred pound man squirm about as he held onto a local branch.

"He's going to fall," Travis commented.

"He might," William agreed, then radioed to Matt. "Hey partner, you ought to come find us in this grove. I have something for you to see." He chuckled, then focused in on Billy Boobs and spoke loudly, "You can't stay up there forever."

"Well . . . you guys go home," he bellowed, "then I'll come down."

"We can't do that Billy. You failed to make your court appearance so now you have to come with us."

"I can't do that either then!" he shouted down to him.

William took a picture of the fugitive with his cell phone.

Two minutes later and Matt arrived on foot to see their bounty in a tree. "How in the hell did he get up there?" he asked in amazement as he glanced at the gang, then back up at the large man.

The crew just shrugged their shoulders.

"We need a ladder," Nick suggested in between taking drags.

"The fire department has one," Travis replied.

"You hear that?" William yelled upward, "You want the fire department to bring their ladder so they can escort your big ass down out of that tree? I'd be pretty embarrassed if I were you!"

Billy was silent.

"It's either us or them Billy and I recommend that you come down out of that tree for us."

"We're not going away," Matt added to William's warning.

"I don't have any reason to come down. Lisa is gone."

William turned and spoke briefly to his crew. "Woman troubles."

Just then, they heard the cracking sound of a limb. They all quickly cast their sights upward and saw the large branch yield to the weight of the gigantic man.

"Oh shit!" the group exclaimed.

The limb snapped, sending Billy on a downward drop. He tumbled, making contact with the branches until he crash landed onto a bush. He lay idle.

William stepped within the large plant and as he visually inspected for any injuries, he handcuffed his wrists together. "Where do you hurt?" he asked him in a rough manner even though he really didn't care.

Billy just moaned.

"I'm calling an ambulance." Matt dipped his free hand into his pocket and extracted his cell phone. He turned himself around as he began to dial nine one one, William advised him that Billy was okay.

The rain dampened their mood to work on the yard even after the droplets had ceased and the sky became blue once again. Luke fell asleep on the couch and Reddy went to his bedroom to read a book.

Nathan was bored playing video games. He stretched as he arose from the love seat, then left the living room, stepping out onto the front porch. He scanned the area and saw a rabbit hopping across the dirt lane until it stopped at a mud puddle for a drink. "That's awesome," he spoke to himself.

He walked quietly towards it, trying to get as close to it as he could before it jumped away. When he neared the end of the driveway, another rabbit came springing from the brush and joined the first cottontail for a taste of the dirty water. Nathan crept in closer. At about ten feet away, he stopped and knelt so he could watch them lap and wiggle their noses.

Soon the rabbits ran off because Critter advanced.

Nathan stood. "Oh . . . you scared them off."

"I'm sorry."

"That's okay, I'd rather watch you anyways."

"Watch me do what?"

He grinned. "Anything you wanna do."

With a timid smile, she took hold of the hem of her skirt and enacted a few twirls, then gently swayed her hips side to side.

"Girl—you got it going on!" he roared, then stepped in, wrapped his arms around her tiny waist, and lifted her up to his chest.

She giggled.

He placed her back onto the ground, then cast his eyes at the house before returning his attention to her. "I thought about what you asked me. If we take the bus, we might get caught before I can get you to your grandmother's house."

"What do you suggest then?" she asked.

Before he could answer, his attention was diverted to a movement in a bush, however it didn't sound like a fluffy bunny. "We should get in the house."

"Whatever it is, my brothers will scare it off."

They turned themselves toward the house and after taking a few steps, they stopped suddenly because a spotted mountain lion cub had appeared before them. It attempted to roar with its budding vocals, then a second cub came pouncing from the shrubbery and joined it for play.

"Oh crap!" Nathan grabbed Critter's hand and in a forceful manner, he guided her away. "Mama lion is very near."

"But they're so cute!" she remarked.

"Mama will kill you Critter," he warned. While they walked the dirt lane, it seemed as though the house was a half a mile away. Nathan's heart was pounding; he knew the full grown mountain lion could spring on them anytime. He wished he had Sandy's machete about now.

They were almost to the rear of Reddy's truck when Critter turned her head around and saw the mama lion advancing their way. "She's coming!"

Nathan took a glance at the gray colored feline. "Get in the truck!" he thundered as they dashed for the doors.

Critter opened her side and jumped in, however, Nathan's door was locked. After she closed her door and noted that Nathan couldn't obtain entry, she hastened to the passenger's side to let him in, but he had already ran around to her side.

Nathan pulled open the metal structure and as he hopped upon the seat, the lion leaped onto the hood.

Critter screamed.

Nathan quickly closed his door, then honked the horn. "Are they still cute?" he shouted to his girlfriend as the honking and screaming continued.

"Don't yell at me!" She was almost in tears.

"What the hell?" Reddy exclaimed as he awoke from a sleep and aimed himself for the front porch. His yawn was interrupted and his eyes widened when he saw the large cat on his truck. He quickly turned and ran back into the house, to his bedroom where he grabbed his rifle.

"Run Mama lion!" Critter urged in a powerful voice, "before you get shot!"

Reddy returned to the porch, went down the steps, and fired the gun into the air causing the dangerous animal to bail to the ground.

Nathan and Critter watched the mountain lion return to her cubs and disappear into the forest. When they thought it was safe, they exited the truck and advanced to the hood where Critter placed her hand onto a muddy paw print and compared the size.

Nathan took a peek at Reddy who had withdrew himself into the house, then cast his eyes to an old shed that was buried within the trees and covered with moss. "What's in there?" he asked his girlfriend.

"Just our snowmobile and a four-wheeler."

CHAPTER THIRTEEN

Somatic Disturbances

"Does it run?" Nathan sought, hoping for a positive reply of the all-terrain vehicle.

"I think so. Luke and Reddy rode on it just last summer," Critter answered before they entered into the house from the front porch. She stepped into the kitchen where Reddy was searching through the cupboards. "Can Nathan come into my room and listen to music with me?"

"Maybe after dinner." He pulled a can of pork n' beans and a bag of chips from the shelf.

"Are you still going to barbecue hot dogs?" she asked.

"Luke's firing up the grill now."

She had been depressed because Matt didn't much encourage or praise her for any reason or occasion. Without him knowing, Dominique dabbed a tear onto her pillow as she lay face down, trying to enjoy his small rubs upon her back. She wondered if he was being sincere with his touches or if he had other motives in mind.

The next fifteen minutes was rare, but nice; the back rub and then the sex.

Later that day, after dinner, Dominique relaxed in front of the living room tv with her writings, but couldn't concentrate much. With Nathan on her mind, she glanced over at Ian who had sat on the opposite side of the couch with his portable video game system.

She soon scribbled a few words, almost creating a sentence when Matt entered the room, stepped to her, and bent down to kiss her atop of her head.

"Do you need anything at the store?" he asked.

"No." She thought on that for a moment after he left. She presumed he was going for beer and now she knew why he had been so nice to her earlier.

The hot dogs and beans took care of his hunger pains. Nathan looked down at his popped belly and knew it wouldn't last. He was only allowed to eat once a day and with the yard work he had already done, he had lost weight. Critter tried to sneak him snacks; pie, cookies, or crackers, however, it wasn't every day.

Nathan was seated Indian style on Critter's bedroom floor upon the carpet next to her. She was showing him photos of her family and of herself when she was younger. "This one is of me and my Pa on his old motorcycle. Wasn't I cute?"

After he eyed the photo, his thoughts wandered to the all-terrain vehicle that is supposably in the shed.

The music played from Critter's small boom box on low volume because she had to keep the door open.

Nathan leaned aside and whispered into her ear. "I'm gonna sneak out to the shed and check out the four-wheeler."

She expressed a sense of alarm. "Why?"

"You want to go to your grandma's, right?"

"Yea."

"Well . . . we could ride on it until we roll into Pinehurst."

"I don't know if there's enough gas in it," she deemed.

"I'll find out."

After Reddy checked on Nathan and Critter, he returned to the living room where he resumed playing Alienoids with Luke.

Nathan glanced at Critter's open window, then at her. "Do you have a flashlight?"

"We do . . ." she answered with much thought, "but I think it's in the truck."

"Great," he remarked with sarcasm. He arose to his feet and went to the open doorway for a listen before heading to the window. As he quietly removed the screen that Reddy had recently installed, Critter joined him. "Go close the bathroom door," he told her, "If your brothers look in on us, you could tell them I'm taking a long shit."

"That's gross!" she spoke in a disgusted, but low voice.

After Nathan climbed over the ledge and jumped to the ground, Critter tiptoed through the hall and closed the bathroom door just as he had suggested. She returned to her room and while she waited for her boyfriend, she changed the compact disc in her boom box to a different artist.

Nathan soon appeared at the window. "It's locked."

She thought for a second, then with an upward index finger, she gestured for him to wait a minute. She left her bedroom and returned shortly after. "I had to sneak into Pa's bedroom. I hope it's the right key." She handed it to him.

He sent her a tiny kiss through the air with his lips, then hustled alongside the house, between a few trees and shrubbery before coming to the old mossy shed. He veered his eyes toward the house to make sure it was clear, then rounded the corner of the small building and stepped to the door. He inserted the key into the padlock and twisted. "Yes—it worked!"

He removed the padlock and when he pushed on the door, it creaked. He stepped in and had to let his eyes adjust as he scanned the miscellaneous objects. He saw a snowmobile, a broken down motorcycle, and an old rowboat before he caught sight of the all-terrain vehicle parked over by the larger entry. He hastened forward and looked it over. "It looks like it will run."

He observed that the tires were filled with enough air, then he fiddled with the handlebars and brakes. He unscrewed the gas cap and checked to see how much liquid was inside the tank. He pushed on the vehicle a few times to hear only a little sloshing. He stepped about the area, searching for a fuel can. He found two containers that had been placed in a corner amongst oil tins. He leaped forward and lifted the cans. The smaller one was empty, but the five gallon can was half full. He chuckled. "Finders keepers Bitches! This vehicle is mine now."

Nathan quickly examined where the handles and locks on the larger entry door were, then left the shed. He refastened the padlock to the door and after taking a few steps past the edge of the shed, he saw through the heavy growth, Reddy coming his way. "How the hell does he know?" he uttered to himself.

He darted behind a tree, then dashed toward another. He tried keeping his sights on his jailer as he continued to slink back toward Critter's window.

"Nathan?" Reddy called out, "I know you're out here."

He didn't answer.

"Where are you?"

Nathan sensed Reddy's tone was sounding more angry as he came closer, however, he kept moving away from him through the brush. Within the minute, he arrived at the window. He placed his hands onto the sill and after he hoisted himself up, he felt two hands grab onto the back of his shirt and pull him down.

The sun was touching the mountain top after a long hot day when Dominique and Ian emerged from their indoor swimming pool, leaving Rainy and Adam to swim alone. They patted themselves with a towel, put their robes on, then headed to their separate bedrooms to shower and change.

Matt was in the master bedroom drinking his beer and watching television. He didn't like to swim.

Dominique turned the doorknob and as she opened the door, she noticed Matt changing the channel rather quickly. "Why'd you change the channel?" she asked him.

"I was watching this," he slurred.

That's a dumb answer, she thought, knowing it wasn't even on commercial. "If you're watching this, why'd you have it on another channel?"

He just sat quiet in his drunkin' stupor, watching the show.

She stepped toward him, grabbed the remote control out of his hand and pushed the recall button. On the screen appeared a blonde woman with bare breasts walking in a field. She pushed the recall button again, then threw the remote at him. "Why can't you come to me when you're feeling nasty? I'd let you look and play with my boobs?"

He didn't answer.

She was feeling hurt as she stood beside the bed eyeing him. She knew it was because her body wasn't a perfect ten like the centerfolds or exotic starlets, but still she thought, it was disrespectful and unfaithful of him to secretly want other women.

This wasn't the first time she caught Matt in the midst of lust. Something inside her clicked. As she glared at him, her face became red and her heart began to thump. She took her robe off. She tightened her lips together and as she bent her fingers up into her palms, she lunged toward him. Tired of being unwanted, ignored, or just plain used, she swung her fists repetitiously.

"Hit me—go ahead and hit me!" Matt roared as he let her smack upon him because he didn't believe in hitting women.

After a round of about thirty hits to his face and chest, she was worn out. As she arose from the bed, she noted the red marks and the blood on his lip. She turned and as she walked away, she observed Ian standing with the door ajar, staring at them.

"I'll be out in a bit," she told her spying son.

He stepped back and closed the door.

"What are you doing sneaking about out here?" Reddy yelled.

"I wasn't sneaking about," Nathan claimed, "I was just looking for a flower for Critter."

"You expect me to believe that?"

"Yes." He knew his excuse sounded corny.

"Did you find one?" He glanced down at Nathan's hands.

"No."

"That's because you weren't really lookin' for one!" He increased the intensity in his voice to see if Nathan would say anything different.

"You'll believe what you want to believe."

Reddy reached forward, grabbed Nathan by his shirt collar, and pulled him in close. "Are you being a smartass?"

"I'm not meaning to be."

He let go of his shirt and as he stepped back, he became aware that Nathan's fist was closed. "What's in your hand?"

"Nothing." He presented and held open his hand.

"Your other hand?"

Nathan knew he was caught. He should have put the key in his pocket after leaving the shed.

"Where did you get this key?" Reddy barked.

Critter stuck her head out her window. "Leave him alone—I gave it to him."

"Why?" Her brother asked her.

"He wanted to see Pa's old motorcycle."

Reddy studied Nathan with curiosity. "Did you see it?"

"I didn't make it that far," he fabricated.

"Don't be nosin' around where it don't belong!" he warned as he took the key from him, then turned his attention to Critter. "Put your screen back on." He grabbed Nathan by his arm and forced him toward the front of the house.

"No need for pushing," Nathan spoke in protest.

"I'll push if I want to," Reddy thundered, then shoved him again.

Nathan brought to mind his karate training, wanting to give him a roundhouse to the face. With little space between the house and the bushes, he could only lift his leg and execute a sidekick.

Reddy soared backwards, landing on his rear. "You mother-fucker!" he yelled after he gained composure.

Nathan dashed away to the front porch with Reddy chasing him. He turned himself quickly and dropped down onto the swing, then hoisted his legs into the air in defense. "Leave me alone!"

Reddy halted. He stood and eyed him briefly, then laughed. "Okay turd, you win this time. I'll leave you outside with the mountain lions."

Nathan watched him walk into the house and close the door. He heard him lock it. After some ten minutes, he laid back on the swing and looked up at the sky. When he noted the first star of the night, he made a wish. "I wish I could go home," he whispered.

He was soon interrupted by a knock on the living room window. He cast his eyes to the side and saw Reddy standing on the inside of the house, taking a toke from a joint.

Reddy was smiling. While he held in his hit, he moved the marijuana stick around, flaunting it.

Nathan had calmed down and returned the grin as he sat up. "Are you going to share?" he asked through the window.

Reddy shook his head no and took another toke.

"Come on Bitch—share!"

Two hours had passed and the movie finished with a sad ending. The lighting in the room was dim accompanied by a haze of smoke that drifted about. Critter wiped her tear, hoping Nathan or her brothers didn't see.

"Well . . . I'm going to bed." Luke yawned and stretched before arising to his feet. He stepped to the front door and locked it, setting the device to his homemade alarm.

"I'm beat too." Reddy waited and after Critter said her good nights, he followed behind her to their separate bedrooms.

Nathan went to his blue couch and laid down. He had his eyes closed for only a minute when he sensed he had to pee. He advanced to his feet, walked through the dark hallway, and when he approached the bathroom door, he heard Luke and Reddy's voices. Curiosity caught his attention when he heard his name so he stepped to the edge of the door frame and listened.

"Next week you'll have to take care of your little problem," Luke advised him, "Pa will be coming home."

"I'll tell him I'm taking him for a hike to see some marijuana plants and do away with him," Reddy stated, "Ain't nobody gonna find him in the wilderness. I'll tell Critter he somehow escaped and went home during the night."

Nathan choked down the lump in his throat, then stepped into the bathroom.

Dominique chuckled as she sat on the floor in the near dark beside her son's empty bed. She just finished praying for his safe return when she remembered how he use to pray when he was younger. She recalled that he would ask the Lord to protect him from earthquakes, hurricanes, and tornadoes even though Idaho didn't have those certain natural disasters. Fires, floods, explosions, murderers, and water pipes bursting were a few more.

CHAPTER FOURTEEN

The One Who Got Away

Even though his future looked grim if he didn't escape was on his mind, Nathan was thankful for a full night's rest because Reddy and Luke were working him like a dog. The back yard was close to being done: The trees were trimmed, the overgrowth was cut, and the rocks and rubbish had been removed. He finished painting the fence and was on a break. As he sat on a chair within the shaded back porch with his lemonade, he peeled the dry paint splatters from his hands.

Critter joined him with her lemonade in the other chair. "Reddy said if you go in the house, he'll get you stoned."

"I'm out of here," he replied, figuring he was still safe.

"Wait!" She grabbed onto his arm before he could stand up. "I wanted to tell you something."

"Huh?" He quickly recalled Luke and Reddy's conversation.

She leaned towards his ear and whispered. "My bags are packed."

He looked at her with relief, yet still wondering. "Bags? How many bags do you have woman?"

She giggled. "A backpack and a large duffel bag that I'll carry."

"Okay . . ." he hesitated when the thought of her holding onto it while riding on the back end of the four-wheeler came to his mind. "We still need that key Reddy took."

"I'll work on it Babe."

"Don't get caught." He tapped her atop of the head with his hand, then walked into the house.

Matt wasn't wearing his arm sling when he exited his bedroom for the day. He went straight to the medicine cabinet for some pain relievers.

"Good afternoon Uncle Matt! Not felling very well?" Rainy asked him as she passed by the open doorway.

"Just a little headache," he replied, then walked with her to the kitchen. Rainy sat at the table with Adam and Travis while Matt grabbed a pepsi from the refrigerator and headed through the back door, by-passing his wife.

Dominique observed his snub and left the room.

Travis followed his mom, ending his steps at her bedroom door. He saw that she was collecting Matt's empty beer bottles and setting them in the plastic garbage can she carried. "It stinks in here," he remarked.

She sighed heavily as she sat onto the edge of her bed. "I'm starting to hate being married to him."

"I think I would too if I were you," he tried to comfort her.

Matt went to the garage where he smoked on a cigarette as he eyed the lawn mower. He thought he'd give mowing a try in spite of his bruised arm.

He had only mowed a small section when William approached him, wearing a grin. "I see your arm is better?"

Matt cut the engine. "It's hurting some. What's up?"

"Swade has a client who quit calling in. We need to go find him."

"I'll gather the crew and meet you at the office."

After Matt put the lawn mower back in the garage, he went into he house. Everyone had cleared the kitchen except for Rainy who was on the telephone.

She had just finished her call. "I got a job Uncle Matt. I went into the veterinary clinic like you suggested. It's only part-time, but I'll be helping to wash the animals and take them outside to poop!"

"Awesome. That's really great!"

"I've also filled out the paperwork for a grant so I can start college this fall. Little Joshy will be almost eight years old when I graduate and become a veterinarian."

"Sounds like you have a lot of work ahead of you," he remarked, then politely inquired Adam's whereabouts.

Matt didn't kiss Dominique good bye. He figured he would just wait for her to approach him when she felt like it even if it meant waiting a few days. God forbid he apologize and try to make things right, he recalled Dominique's statement from a previous argument, but right now, he didn't care. He attempted to get her off his mind as he turned his attention to what William was saying.

"His name is Lenny Silks. He's twenty-five years old, five feet nine, a hundred and sixty pounds."

"Just an average sized man this time boys," Matt stated.

William nodded, then turned to Travis. "What's his criminal record look like?"

Travis read from his file. "Petty theft, another petty theft, illegal possession of drugs and drug paraphernalia, second degree assault."

"Second degree assault, huh? Does it say what kind of weapon he used?"

"A rock."

"He's a scrapper. I bet there's an interesting story behind that one."

"Oh . . . here we go," Travis read, "Burglary with the use of deadly force."

"Yap, Lenny's dangerous," William spoke firmly, "and he's runnin' because he knows he's on his way to prison for a few years."

"The co-signer," Matt proceeded, "for this bond is his girlfriend, Dary. I suggest we gear up and go to her place first."

"I agree," William said.

They soon hopped into the SUV's and drove to Coeur d' Alene to Fifteenth Street. Travis and Adam took their positions in the back yard while William and Matt approached and knocked at the front door.

With a cigarette in hand, Dary stepped out onto the patio. "He's not here. We broke up last week."

"We've been getting that a lot."

William ignored Matt's comment. "Do you know where we can find him?" he asked her.

"Nope and I don't care." She took a drag from her cigarette. "He lied to me one too many times."

"You're his co-signer, you need to care."

"I asked Swade to take me off the bond."

"After we catch him he can." He showed her Lenny's picture. "Is this how he still looks?"

"No. He cut his hair and shaved his mustache off so he don't singe it while he's smoking his crack."

After searching Dary's house, the bounty hunters left with the name and address of Lenny's best friend Mark, but their next stop would be his place of employment.

William and Travis talked to the manager of the pizza restaurant, then exited the building and informed Matt and Adam that Lenny had been fired from his job last week.

"Let's go to Mark's house."

Some ten minutes later and they were knocking at Mark's door.

"No one's home," William radioed to the crew.

Matt and Adam who were keeping watch from the back porch, peeked in through the kitchen window and saw dirty dishes and rubbish strewn about the counter tops and table. "It's filthy in there."

Matt backed away from the window, stepped to the door, and tested the knob. "It's unlocked!" he buzzed to Adam as he slowly opened the door. He poked his head in. "Hello?" he hollered, then with no reply, he walked in.

"Are you crazy?" Adam asked, yet followed behind his uncle, holding onto a large can of pepper spray.

Matt shined his flashlight into the dark corners as he quickly searched throughout the different rooms.

"Come on dude, this is trespassing," Adam who was fearful, spoke.

"Wait a sec." Matt stopped at the coffee table and skimmed through some loose papers. He found on a small piece of ripped paper, Lenny's name and an address, yet it wasn't the address in their file. "How lucky is this?" he chuckled as he showed it to Adam.

CUCKOO-CUCKOO!

Adam gasped, then turned and spotted a cuckoo clock. "That thing scared the shit out of me!"

"I know. I saw you jump," Matt was grinning as he spoke.

They both walked to the rear door and exited.

"Where are you two at?" William grumbled over the radio.

"Right behind you," Matt replied, then after his partner turned around, he handed him the piece of paper.

William read it. "Good work. Let's go check it out." They returned to their SUV's and drove away.

They traveled only five blocks before arriving at the specific locality. As they stepped away from their vehicles, they scanned the refined property. The vista of scenery was beautiful, composed of many rows of flowers surrounded by wooden chips that covered the ground. The lush green lawn contained two cottonwood trees, one on each side of the yard.

They walked the sidewalk toward the front door while Matt and Adam hustled around to the back yard to again stand guard.

"You wouldn't think a crackhead would live in a nice place like this," William remarked to Travis, then knocked.

"It's probably a parent or grandparent who lives here."

Soon the door opened and a man with facial features resembling Lenny appeared. "Yes?" he asked with a firm tone.

"Hello Sir," William spoke politely, "I'm looking for Lenny Silks. Is he here?"

The man observed their garb and especially the badges. "No. And please, just leave him alone!"

"We can't just leave him alone. He quit calling and checking in with his bail bondsman so we need to find him. Are you his father?"

"Of course I am. Who else would I be?" he snapped.

William didn't respond to his rude question. "Do you know where he is? Where I can find him?"

"Would you expect me to tell you if I did?"

"That would be the best thing for you to do," William urged.

"No it wouldn't," Lenny Senior grumbled, "He'll just wait until the statute of limitations runs out on his charges, then he'll be safe to return."

"Oh wow!" Matt reacted.

"Listen," the father disclosed, "He was a good kid until . . . he is a good kid who's had a rough life since his mama and brother died four years ago in an automobile accident."

"I can understand that Sir," William sympathized with him, "but maybe you don't realize he's smoking ice and will probably get into more trouble if he doesn't get help."

"He's a smart guy, he'll eventually figure it out."

"Don't be stupid!" He felt himself becoming irritated with this man. "Tell us where he is!"

Lenny Senior stepped back and shut his front door rather hard.

Matt looked at William with surprise. "Now what?"

William banged on the door with his fist. "Help us find your son!" he roared, "Your cooperation is greatly needed."

In a short time, with the chain guard in place, the man cracked open the door. "He's decided to live as a homeless person in Spokane. Please help him bounty hunter." He closed the door.

Nathan tossed the grass seed, letting it scatter onto the dirt in the back yard. He then raked the seeds within the loose soil before spraying a small amount of water upon the ground. As he did this sowing, he knew the yard work was near completion and Reddy would be wanting to deal with him. He cast his eyes about the yard trying to come up with something he could do or add to it while he stalled for time.

"It's lookin' pretty good back here!" Reddy remarked as he stepped in beside his cheap toiler.

Nathan was startled by his presence. "Oh . . . yea," he agreed.

After a moment of gazing, Reddy returned to the inside of the house.

Nathan finished watering and was straightening the patio of gardening tools and garbage when Critter joined him. "What's up?" he asked her.

She hesitated, but finally spoke. "I didn't find any keys yet, but I did find a condom." She held it out for him to see.

"Put that away!" he emphasized within a whisper. "If your brothers saw you with that, they'd hurt me real good."

"I wouldn't let them."

"You couldn't stop them Critter."

She was silent as she heeded to her thoughts. "How long should I keep it put away for?"

He stopped what he was doing and eyed her. "For a while." He ached having to tell her that because as a young man, he would love to take her here and now. "Maybe on our way to your grandmother's house we can stop somewhere."

She blushed, then walked into the house.

Two days later, William Hoffman returned to Kellogg after posing as a homeless man on the streets of Spokane. He joined the crew at the office to tell them about his quest. "Where's Adam?" he asked Matt and Travis.

"He's in Spokane taking his written exam."

"Good—I hope he passes." He paced the floor. "I showed Lenny's photo around to various men including the staff at the shelter, some knew him, some didn't. A few fellows gave me different information saying he left with someone who was heading to Seattle, but that person was still at the mission. The conclusion of this hunt, I think, is that Lenny left Spokane three days ago by himself." He sat at his desk.

"He's the one who got away," Travis growled, "Swade is not going to be happy at all."

"I sure feel like an Underdog today," Matt remarked sadly.

"Cheer up—I have a brother who lives in Tacoma. Let me call him, then I'll be on my way there," William posed, "We'll get him!"

She couldn't stand his silent treatment any longer even though she knew he should be the one to apologize and make things better between them. She'd have to be the one to break the ice again.

After Matt came home from meeting with William, he stepped in the kitchen where Dominique was removing hot pans of cinnamon rolls from the oven. "Smells good in here."

She cast her eyes upon him. "Wow! You're going to talk to me?"

"Yea, why wouldn't I?"

She gave him a strange look. "You've been avoiding me for three days."

He just leaned against the counter.

"I have some things I do need to say to you, but you probably won't like them." She tossed her oven mits onto the counter.

He rolled his eyes, but not so she could see.

She grabbed her cigarettes and lit one. "I think it would be best for everyone if you quit drinking."

"I don't want to quit drinking."

"It causes too much trouble for us. I've tried telling you this before."

He didn't reply.

"Don't you care about our marriage?"

"I care."

"You sure don't show it." She took a drag from her cigarette. "Don't you think it hurts my heart when you drool over other women?"

"I don't drool."

"You're quite the bastard Matt." She walked away to the back patio where she finished her cigarette, accompanied by a few tears. She was waiting, but not expecting him to come after her and tell her she was the most beautiful woman in his eyes or to sweep her off her feet with spontaneous words of love.

CHAPTER FIFTEEN

The Key To Freedom

There was a knock at the front door. Dominique adjusted the volume on the television and stepped into the entryway. When she opened the door, a young redheaded teenage boy stood beside her flower pot.

"Is Nathan here?"

"Oh wow," she mumbled to herself. She thought it was odd for him to be asking since the word of Nathan's disappearance was all over town. "Who are you?" she asked.

"Brian Jay."

"Why do you want Nathan, may I ask?"

"He was going to sell me a video game."

"When did you last talk to him?" she spoke with anticipation.

"About a month ago," he replied, "before I went on vacation."

"Where did you last see him?"

"Um . . . at the park. He didn't have the game with him then so he told me he'd sell it to me later cuz he was leaving with Critter and some guy."

"Oh my gosh!" she exclaimed with teary eyes. "Nathan's not home now, but I'll tell him you were here." She closed the door and went running into her bedroom where Matt was watching television.

He eyed her with wonder.

She dashed to the dresser and grabbed her car keys. "Come on—I have a clue at where Nathan might be. I have to go see Detective Morris."

Critter rushed into the kitchen with soft foot steps and halted beside Nathan who was drying the dinner dishes. "I've got Luke's truck key." She opened her palm to show him.

His heart began to beat fast as he observed and took hold of it. He hadn't expected the truck key, but it was a nice surprise and he knew how to drive, however, he hadn't a driver's license yet. He looked up at her. "Should we go now?"

"Yes!" she demanded.

He cast a furtive glance through the doorway of the living room, then back towards the hallway.

"Luke's in the shower and Reddy's laying on his bed," she whispered.

His mind went racing with different thoughts. "You go grab your bags and get in the truck, then I'll run out there and we'll leave." His throat went dry. "And don't forget your money!"

While Critter went to her bedroom, he continued to dry a dish or two, hoping not to drop a plate. His imagination wandered to the starting of Luke's truck. What if it didn't start right away and Reddy heard the sputtering and came running out of the house with his rifle? He took in a deep breath as he stared at the front entry. His feet were itching to step toward and out that door for the last time, then he gave ear to Luke turning off the shower. "Hurry up Critter," he mumbled.

Within the minute, Critter carried two pieces of luggage and her pillow through the open doorway.

Nathan tossed the dishtowel onto the counter and walked out of the kitchen, through the living room, then met up with his girl on the porch. He seized her suitcase and hastened for the truck. "I thought you said a duffel bag?"

"I repacked last night and needed something bigger."

He hoisted the suitcase into the bed while Critter did the same with her backpack. "Don't shut the door yet," he told her from across the vehicle.

They jumped into the cab. With sweaty palms, Nathan inserted the key into the firing mechanism, then glanced up at the house. Seeing that it was still clear, he turned the ignition. He could hardly breathe.

Reddy heard the truck's engine start. He knew Luke was in the bathroom so he hopped from his bed and headed toward the front of the house.

Nathan pressed on the brake and set the gear into reverse. He backed out, turning the truck's direction. He braked again and after he put it in drive, the engine stalled and died. "Oh Nathan—You idiot!" he scolded himself aloud.

"Try again," Critter begged.

He had already moved the indicator to neutral and was turning the key. After some sputtering, it started.

Critter spun her head around and looked out the rear window. "Reddy's coming!" she shouted, "Go!"

As fast as he could, he shifted into drive and pressed on the accelerator. As he peeled out, Reddy banged on the driver's window.

"Stop this truck now!" he thundered, "Critter, you get out!" He tried to grab onto the rim of the truck and jump in the bed, but as the vehicle moved forward, he slipped and fell; his arm barely missing the path of the rear tire.

Nathan sped upon the dirt lane, following where it led. He looked in his rear view mirror and saw Reddy standing to his feet, then run toward the house. He cast his eyes onto the gauges and noted the gas gauge was on E. "Oh shit!" He glanced at the road, then at Critter. "How many miles until we get to town?"

"Maybe ten or twelve."

When Reddy ran into the house, Luke was combing his hair. "Did you see that?" he asked his brother with urgency. "Nathan just drove off with Critter."

"They won't get far on an empty tank. Go put the spare gas in the four-wheeler."

Reddy first ran to his bedroom and grabbed his large hunting knife. He inserted his belt through the eyelets in his sheath and as he advanced outside to the old mossy shed, he strapped his belt on.

Luke stashed his weed within his mattress, then threw on his shoes and a sweatshirt. He turned off the television and after stepping outside, he closed the door.

Nathan drove the curvy road about two miles and crossed a small wooden bridge made from planks before reaching a paved one-lane road. "Which way?"

"That way." Critter pointed north.

Nathan proceeded upon the old cracked blacktop. On one side of the road was a dirt mountainside with sparse bushes and pine trees and on the other side was a creek. While he drove over the bumpy road, maneuvering around the potholes, he felt the road tipping downward as though he was slowly descending. He knew it would help conserve on the gas.

He glanced down at the gauges. He was traveling at fifty miles per hour and the fuel indicator still read E. Lord, he prayed silently, If you ever let a truck run on fumes, let it be now.

Detective Morris was trying to figure out who Critter was. "It has to be a nickname," he told his partner, Detective Amy.

"I think the first and best place to find out about her would be to obtain her school records."

"Two great minds think alike," he remarked, "I'll call the principal at his home and have him meet us at the school. They'll have her address and parents' names as well."

"We'll crack this case yet and find that boy!"

After the phone call, the two detectives left Wallace and drove to Kellogg to the high school. Without knowing it, they were being followed.

With Adam on board, Travis turned onto the dead end street that led to the school. He drove past the hospital and steered into its parking lot. He parked near the exit and used his cell phone to call his mother with a situation report.

"I want to know their every move, keep me posted," Dominique said at the conclusion of the call.

"Let's see . . ." the principal spoke as he opened the files on the computer. "I don't recall having a student named Critter."

Detective Morris suggested it was a nickname.

"Let me call my secretary." As he remained at his desk, he lifted the receiver on the telephone and dialed. "Hi Mary. Just a quick question for you. I have two detectives here with me in the school's office and I need to know if there is a student by the name of Critter?"

"Yes, I know her," she answered, "Christina Meyer. She's a quiet one, but always came into the office claiming to be sick."

"Thanks Mary. Enjoy the rest of your summer break."

The detective's listened and waited while the principal typed in her name.

"Her mom is listed as deceased, but her father's name is Luke Meyer Senior."

"So she has a sibling out there somewhere named Luke Junior, huh?" Amy reckoned.

The principal glanced at the detectives. "I'll look him up next. He probably was a student here too." He continued to read from Critter's file. "Oh wow! She lives way up the creek up on the last dirt road." He cast his eyes upon them. "I would recommend getting a hold of the bus driver if you don't know that area. He or she will be able to tell you where her bus stop is or if they even drive up that far."

"Thank you so much for your time and help," Amy told him, then turned to her partner. "Let's head to Pinehurst."

Nathan was somewhat relieved when he read a sign that said Pinehurst city limits. He observed the houses that bordered the small town as well as the large church to his left as he rounded the last bend in the curvy road. The truck began to sputter, then the engine died. He steered the truck to the side of the road. "Thank God!" he praised as he cast his vision onto the gauges, however, he knew he was still in danger.

"What are we going to do now" Critter asked with worry.

He quickly spied the area and saw a small paved street that ran alongside a grove of trees on the hillside. "We're definitely not going to stay here in the cab of this truck. I'll bet you anything that your brothers hopped on the four-wheeler and are only five minutes or so behind us."

"You could be right."

They exited Luke's truck and grabbed the luggage.

"We have to stash your bags somewhere and come back for them after we get another vehicle."

They were walking on the side street nearing the grove of trees when Nathan stopped suddenly and gaped at Critter. "Do you hear that?" He turned and glanced back at the truck.

"It's our four-wheeler!" She exhibited fear.

"Come on!" They hustled some ten yards, then veered toward the hillside into some bushes and pine trees. Nathan fell in the ditch mostly atop of her suitcase, hurting his knee. "Damn it!" he vented silently.

"Are you okay?" she asked.

He knew there wasn't time now to inspect his injury, so he stood to his feet and led Critter to a camouflaged area where they sat down together. He then inspected his left knee and rubbed it. "It's not cut or bleeding, it's just sore."

"I'm glad it's not bleeding."

"Shh . . . no talking or moving now—even if you see a bug or spider," he cautioned as he looked in the direction of Luke's truck. "If Luke or Reddy spot us, I'm running and you'll never see me again."

"Oohh . . ." she whined as she rested her head onto the side of his arm.

"I'd have to Critter. They wanted to take me somewhere and do away with me."

When Luke and Reddy arrived at the truck, they anxiously jumped off their all-terrain vehicle. Luke looked inside the cab while Reddy peeked in the bed. "There was a suitcase in the back here," he told his twin.

"They can't be very far." He moved his eyes about the neighborhood, searching the sidewalks and streets for his sister. "They're probably walking on the back streets. Let's go get some gas first, then we can track them down."

They remounted onto their ATV and sped down Division Street to the nearby fuel station.

After arriving into the quiet residential town, Detective Morris and Detective Amy drove to the scanty police station where they met up with two policemen.

Travis and Adam parked in a parking lot across from the cop shop with Division Street between them. They watched as the two detectives entered the building.

"What should we do?" Adam asked. "Go in there and demand to know what's going on or just keep following them?"

"That's a good question." Travis remained facing the windshield with his wrinkled brow implying serious thought. "If we don't go in there and we just tail them, we'll have a better chance of getting close to Nathan or his kidnappers. But . . ." He took in a deep breath. "If we go in there and tell them we want to help, they might tell us to leave, that it's only a police matter."

"But we're both certified bounty hunters."

"I don't think I want to chance it. I want to follow them and help rescue my brother."

"You're right."

The detectives introduced themselves to the two Pinehurst law enforcement agents even though they've seen them around at different crime scenes.

"We need your assistance in an investigation regarding the missing seventeen year old boy, Nathan Kiniky," Detective Morris spoke, then continued to explain who they thought had him and where.

"We'd be glad to lead the way," one replied.

They left the brick building and went to their separate police vehicles. The detectives followed the two city cops out of the driveway onto Division Street due south towards Pinecreek.

Travis started his truck's engine, then went in pursuit at a close distance of the law enforcement agents.

CHAPTER SIXTEEN

Groping In The Dark

From the thicket, Nathan watched as Reddy poured fuel from a small red container into the tank of Luke's truck, then he watched him drive their four-wheeler up two metal rails onto the bed of their truck and park it. After securing the ATV with cords, he observed them jumping into the cab and cruise slowly up the back street toward him. "Oh shit!" He knelt while Critter remained perched behind a tree on her suitcase.

As Luke drove past the grove of trees, he switched on his headlights. It was getting dark and harder for him and Reddy to see anyone walking the streets. He traveled to the next block and turned.

Nathan stepped back to Critter. "They're gone."

"You want to smoke my joint now?" she asked.

"Sure," he replied as he sat down next to her. "You just brought all the essentials huh? I bet you even packed the kitchen sink in that suitcase?" he jested, "That's why it's so heavy!" He smiled at her.

"Nathan . . ." she cooed.

Luke and Reddy drove the back streets to the gas station where they finished filling the tank. Once inside the building, while Luke paid for the gas and a drink, Reddy pulled a picture of Critter out from his wallet and showed it to the attendant. "Have you seen her in the last half an hour?"

"No," the man replied after glancing at it.

"We're heading up Pinecreek," Travis reported over his cell phone to his mother as he kept on the police officers' tail. After a few more words were spoken, he ended the call with a promise to check in soon.

He had his headlights radiating on dim while they traveled the narrow strip between the mountainsides and creek. Before long, they came to a fork in the road and instead of turning right over the girder bridge, they drove forward. Travis observed the surroundings; there were no more signs of people nor homesteads, just the wilderness.

"They're going to catch on that we're following them," Adam remarked.

"I know," Travis agreed with a half grin.

The rough gray pavement ended with the road becoming a single dirt lane. Through the dust, Travis crossed over the planks, staying in pursuit, however, he had to press on the brakes when the two city official cars suddenly stopped. "Here we go with the bullshit."

When the two cops stepped past the detective's car, Detective Morris exited and joined them as they walked on toward the strange truck with their flashlights aimed upon Travis and Adam's faces.

"Hello Officers," Travis greeted from the driver's seat.

The lawmen noted the badge that hung about his neck and the black bullet proof vest he wore. "We weren't told you'd be joining us?" one of the cops remarked, waiting for a reply.

He hesitated, "I've just been kind of following on my own."

"Why?"

"Nathan's my brother. I want to help find him."

"Is that so?" The policeman eyed him. "I haven't seen you around before. Where do you work?"

"I'm a bounty hunter for The Underdog's."

"I've heard of them," he replied with thought. "They're a new company, aren't they?"

"Yea. My step dad owns half of it."

"It'll be nice to have more assistance. Let's go—it's getting dark." He tapped the roof of Travis' truck before turning and walking back to his car with his partner.

Travis and Adam were thrilled to be included in the search.

Travis followed as they drove until the lane ended with the only and last house. All was dark and quiet within the residence. They parked, leaving their headlights aglow on bright and exited their automobiles.

Dominique paced the living room floor as she waited anxiously for Travis' next call. She had to keep busy so she went to Nathan's bedroom, stripped the sheets from his bed, and threw them in the washer. While they washed, she dusted his dresser and windowsill, then vacuumed his carpet. "Nathan's coming home!" she told Matt who stepped in by the open doorway to check on her.

"I sure hope so," he tried to ease her anticipation, figuring Nathan's chances were only fifty-fifty.

Nathan decided it was time to go searching for a vehicle. He stood to his feet, took hold of Critter's hand, and with the night upon them, he led her through the grove toward the street. "Whoa!" he laughed as he stumbled, "I can hardly walk."

"Me either," she spoke with a giggle, "I'm so stoned."

Out on the road, Nathan peered up an down the street looking for Luke's white truck. Seeing only the streetlights, they went walking. They walked to the next block, then directed themselves down that certain street.

"I sure hope we can find a car Nathan. I really need to get to my grandma's house."

Grandma . . . he thought. "My grandma lives here in Pinehurst, but I never see her."

"Are you gonna go take her car?"

"I wouldn't want to."

"Yea," she agreed, "I wouldn't want to steal from my grandma either."

Nathan slowed his pace when he came upon a parked car. He scanned the vicinity; it seemed clear. He placed his hand onto the handle and opened the door. When the dome light came on, he peeked at the ignition and looked above the visor. There was no key, so he quietly shut the door. He and Critter continued on down the street.

At the end of the block was a fenced yard where a vehicle was parked just within the enclosure on the driveway. The fence was made of wood and as tall as six feet. Nathan had Critter wait by the corner while he crept toward the projected car, but before he could step foot onto the concrete slab, he heard the barking of a nearby dog who seemed to be approaching rather quickly.

"Oh shit!" he exclaimed as he stopped in his tracks, then as he turned away, he could hear the rattling of a chain. The dog's chain had come to a pause as though the leash had reached its limit. He breathed a sigh of relief.

At that moment, the porch light came on and the front door of the house was opened.

Nathan leaped behind the car.

The homeowner stepped out. "What's out there boy?" he spoke to his dog.

The canine kept barking.

Nathan wanted to take off running; he should of took off running, he thought, but he didn't want the man to see him and call the police.

The man shined a high beam flashlight at his dog, then at his vehicle and around the yard. "Come here boy!" he called to his pet. "There's nothing out here."

The dog obeyed and sprang to his owner.

"Must be a cat!" he mumbled to his dog as he took him inside the house.

Nathan's injured knee was throbbing from being pressed against the hard ground. He arose slowly to his feet and limped away. He returned to the street corner where he had instructed Critter to wait. She was gone. "Oh great!" he spoke with sarcasm as he scanned the moonlit area. "Critter?" His calls were soft as he walked northbound.

When he arrived at the next street, he saw lights from a vehicle heading his way. Could that be Luke and Reddy? he wondered, causing him to scurry into the nearby yard and conceal himself behind a large tree.

As the vehicle approached, he could see at an angle that it was Luke's white truck with the four-wheeler tucked in the bed. He stood erect, barely breathing while his kidnappers passed by slowly. He soon heard the truck's engine fade as it disappeared onto another street. "Oh Critter—where are you?" he spoke softly.

He stepped out from behind the tree and returned to the blacktop. He cast his eyes to his side and saw Critter retreating from a bush. "Critter!" He hastened toward her. "Why'd you leave?"

"Cuz that man came out and I got scared and then I saw a car pass by so I hid."

He wrapped his arm around her tiny body and led her up the street.

Travis was anxious to find his brother. He and Adam took hold of their flashlights and joined the detectives as they approached the strange unlit house.

"Shouldn't we head to the back?" Adam questioned his partner.

"I don't think anyone is here TO catch running out the back." They turned their attention to what the law enforcement agents were doing.

With his pistol in one hand and a flashlight in the other, Detective Morris stood guard while Amy knocked loudly upon the anterior door of the house. "This is the police—open up!"

Travis and Adam held their positions on one side of the porch, whereas, the two officers occupied the other end.

Amy knocked again. "We're coming in!" She tested the knob; it wasn't locked so she finished turning, then pushed it open. She and Detective Morris shined their flashlights about the dark living room and after they stepped in, the two cops followed them. Amy switched on the house light.

Travis and Adam overtook the open doorway and cast their vision within the enclosure, studying the different objects while Detective Morris, Amy, and one of the cops headed into the hallway toward the bedrooms. There were photos of The Meyer family hanging on the wall so Travis entered and scanned their features to see if he recognized any of them.

In the twins bedroom, Detective Morris found and examined Reddy's rifle. "It's been recently cleaned," he told the cop.

Detective Amy continued on to the kitchen where she opened the back door and flipped on the porch light. She moved her flashlight, inspecting the yard. She could smell the unearthed dirt.

Travis wandered through the kitchen and joined Amy.

"This whole yard is freshly dug up," she remarked, "We're gonna have to call in the canines."

He knew it meant searching for a body; his brother's body. He felt ill to his stomach. He would of never thought such a thing like this would of happened to a member of his family. He ached because he didn't want to report this to his mother.

"We'll have to wait until daylight to do a thorough search," she stated as she turned and looked at him. "You're turning pale!"

He swallowed hard, "I'll be okay."

The group convened into the living room. Travis listened in on the conversation while he stared at the rifle that Detective Morris had confiscated, wondering if that was the murder weapon.

"I counted five beds. The father's, Christina's, Luke and Reddy's, and I bet Nathan slept on this blue couch."

Travis glanced at the sofa.

"I'll gather some hair samples and fingerprints. Please, nobody anything," Detective Amy requested, then went outside to her vehicle to retrieve her forensic's kit.

Detective Morris stepped towards Travis. "Do you recognize anything in here that could have been your brother's?"

He took a second look around the room, then answered no.

Nathan eyed a car from beyond the street as he and Critter sat and rested on the curb. After making sure the surrounding area was clear of people, they stood to their feet and strolled across the blacktop. "If you hear me start it up, jump in." He crept to the driver's door while she went to the passenger's side. When Nathan touched the handle to lift it, an alarm sounded. "Oh crap!" he exclaimed, then with Critter in tow, he took off running down the dark street.

After they rounded the corner, Nathan saw Luke's truck exit from a nearby street and head their way. He halted suddenly, grabbing onto Critter's arm to stop her. "Get down!"

They both dropped down onto their bellies positioning themselves in between a few bushes. As Luke drove closer, the roar of his engine overtook the sound of the faint car alarm. Nathan's heart was pounding for he hoped Luke and Reddy hadn't seen them. He didn't even want to look up.

"That was another close one," Critter spoke after elevating her face to see her brothers cruise down the road. "We need to find a car and get the heck out of here!"

"I agree," Nathan replied as he uplifted himself to his knees.

"Where do you think she's headin to with that boy?" Luke asked Reddy while they traveled upon another side street searching for their younger sister.

"Who knows." Reddy cast a glance at his twin through the darkness. "All I know is that if she's not safely tucked away at home when Pa gets back this weekend, our chances of getting that new motorcycle will not be good."

"Well . . . I suggest we park somewhere with the headlights off and wait for them to walk by, then we snatch her."

"Good idea," Reddy agreed, "but first, let's head home and off-load this four-wheeler and grab us a few bowls to smoke while we wait. It'll take a half hour tops."

"I don't know," Luke replied.

"They're not going anywhere outside of Pinehurst," he spoke arrogantly.

The two city cops received a transmission from dispatch to respond to suspicious characters roaming about Pinehurst. They left the Meyer's residence just as the detectives were finishing up their sample collecting.

"We're out of here too," Amy told Travis and Adam, "but we'll be back at daylight." She switched off the lights and exited the house with her partner closing the door. They went to their vehicles.

Detective Morris stepped to Travis' truck. "Make sure that you're posted off their property," he cautioned, knowing they were going to stand guard throughout the night. "And stay off of it no matter what!"

Travis and Adam climbed into the truck and drove to the end of the dirt lane. Travis parked, then cut the engine and headlights. "I can't see a fuckin' thing!" he remarked as he cast his eyes about the pitch black night.

"Not even the moon," Adam replied from the passenger's seat while he gazed upward through the windshield. "It's blocked by all the mountains."

"Lock your door—just in case." He retrieved his cell phone from his pocket and flipped it open. He read the no service available. "I won't be calling my mom."

Ten minutes had past by when they saw lights from a vehicle out on the main road drawing near.

"I wonder if the detectives forgot something?" Adam questioned.

Travis switched on the parking lights, then decided it would be better to shine the headlights and step out.

Adam joined him.

The bounty hunters waited beside their vehicle with flashlights in hand. The other automobile soon rounded the bend and was upon them. As it slowed, they realized it wasn't the detectives returning. Travis could see the driver through the dim glare of the headlamps. "Hey! You're Reddy?" he called out, shocked to see him.

Luke pressed on the brake. "Who wants to know?"

"A lot of people. Where's Nathan?"

"I don't know what you're talking about," he denied firmly.

"What about your sister? Where is she?"

"She's with our Pa, not that it's any of your business. Now if you'll excuse me, I have to get going."

"Why was Nathan seen leaving the Kellogg park with you last month?" Travis shouted as he watched the suspect accelerate onto the dirt lane toward his house.

"That went well," Adam remarked with sarcasm.

Nathan and Critter came upon a tavern. They stood at the edge of the gravelly acre and with the help from a streetlight, they scoped the parking lot. They observed several vehicles with no visible people.

"There has to be at least one car with the keys in it," Nathan said with a touch of hope.

"Let's go find out."

They advanced cautiously between the vehicles. Nathan opened five different doors and groped the ignitions before finally scoring. He dropped himself onto the driver's seat and turned the key, starting the engine.

Critter entered through the passenger's side, sat on the seat, and closed her door. "Whew-hu! Some drunk bastard's gonna be mad when he comes out of the bar to find his car gone."

Nathan shifted the gear into reverse, backed out, then turned on the headlights as he advanced forward toward the street. "We'll go get your luggage, then head to Rainier." He glanced at the fuel gauge. "It looks like we have a full tank. How awesome is that?"

She sprang across the arm rest and smacked his cheek with a kiss.

CHAPTER SEVENTEEN

Escort Service

They were slouched in the seats with their heads propped against the interior side of the cab.

HONK! HONK!

Travis and Adam were startled out of a sleep and when they opened their eyes, it was daybreak. "Oh shit—we fell asleep!" Travis glanced at Adam who was yawning, then he cast his eyes at the detective's car and saw them waving as they accelerated across the planks, onto the dirt lane toward the Meyer's residence. He continued to watch as two vehicles followed, noting that one was a k-9 unit.

"We suck as bounty hunters!" Adam scolded, "We get an all nighter and we blow it!"

Travis agreed. He turned the key, stating the engine, then sped to catch up to the convoy.

When they arrived at the house, they observed Luke's truck to be nowhere in sight and the law enforcement agents were exiting from their vehicles. The k-9 officer had his dog on a leash eager to do his job.

Travis thought about his mother who was probably worried sick and wondering where he was. He took his cell phone from his pocket and opened it. It still read no service available. As he put his communication device away, he advanced toward the house, then followed the task force to the back yard.

The canine started to nose out the soft ground, walking a top of the grass seeds that Nathan had just sowed the day before.

Travis seemed curious and hastened around to the front of the house when a small diesel truck was heard approaching, then the engine was cut. He saw an unknown man standing beside that vehicle talking to a police officer. He overheard the fellow saying his name is Luke and that this is his house.

The officer briefed him on what they were doing, then asked him where Christina was.

"She's suppose to be here with her brothers."

"That's a lie!" Travis stepped forward with his finger pointed at the father. "Reddy told me just last night that she was with you."

"Calm down," the officer commanded to Travis.

"I've been gone for the past month working in Alaska," Luke Senior explained, "I left Critter here with my twin sons."

Travis turned away. Even though he was lost in thought about where Nathan and that girl could be and why he let himself fall asleep, he continued to eye the dad.

"I'll make some calls," Luke told the cop, "I'll be back." He stepped to his house and climbed the trellis. He sat up on the housetop with his cell phone.

Travis returned to the back yard and stood close to Adam and the detectives. The k-9 agent and his dog were done probing, leaving the ground full of depressed feet and paw prints.

"There's no sign of any human remains," the k-9 officer stated to the detectives and bounty hunters, then escorted the dog back to his vehicle.

"That's good news, but it still leaves Nathan missing," one of the detectives replied.

"So where do you go from here?" Travis asked Amy.

"Find the Meyer twins and question them."

Luke Senior rounded the corner of the house and approached them. "My parents haven't seen or heard from them nor their maternal grandmother which is in Texas vacationing. I also dialed Luke's cell phone, but he's out of minutes."

"Do you have any idea where your children are?" Detective Amy questioned as she studied his appearance.

"Like I said, they're suppose to be here."

"I'm going to leave you my card. When," she stressed as she handed him her information, "they come home or you talk to them, call me."

"Will do."

The law enforcement, as well as Travis and Adam, advanced to their vehicles and left the property.

When the rookie informants arrived home, Travis explained their previous twelve hours to Dominique and Matt who were relieved and hoping Nathan was still alive.

"You're never going to live this one down," Matt joked, "Falling asleep on the job?"

"Ha ha!" Travis spoke while everyone smiled.

"You two take the day off, William asked Nick to come in and help us today."

With Ian in Rainy's care, Dominique and Matt left their house to go meet William and Nick.

At the Underdog's office, the team gathered around the table.

"We're going after a prostitute today who disguises herself as an escort," William said as he moved his fingers in bunny ear form. "She violated a restraining order when she snuck into her ex's place to see her daughter." He thumbed through a few papers. "She's also got child endangerment charges and simple assault."

"Simple assault on who? Her children?" Dominique blurted with displeasure in her voice.

Matt just shrugged his shoulders at her.

"Swade said she's a sly one," William continued, "He's also stated that her cell phone's been disconnected so there's no calling her. We'll go to her place of residence before putting plan B into motion."

"Plan B?"

"Yes. We'll trick her out of hiding and that's where Nick comes into the picture. He's going to be our bait, lure her in."

The crew, except for Nick, outfitted themselves in bounty hunting shirts and the proprietors wore badges. All four left the building, climbed into two separate vehicles, and drove to the city.

Once in Coeur d'Alene, they took the Fifteenth Street exit and drove south to Harrison Road. They turned and traveled west until they reached an apartment complex at the end of the city street. They parked alongside the lane next to a fenced cemetery, then stepped out of their SUV's.

"She's in apartment twenty-four."

They were on the property ten minutes when they were told by the manager that Candy had broken her arm in a fight with a neighbor and no longer lived there.

"Hmm . . ." William expressed concern. "There's no record of her going to jail for that?"

"I don't know if the cops were called or not. I wasn't here."

"They should have been."

"Maybe," he spoke as he shrugged his shoulders. "All I can tell you is that I had too many complaints about her so I had to evict her."

"Do you have a forwarding address on her by chance?"

"No."

"Thanks for your time Sir," William acknowledged as the team turned away and headed back to their vehicles.

"She should be easier to spot in a crowd with a cast on her arm," one commented.

William led the way toward downtown, drove Sherman Avenue and soon steered his truck into the parking lot of a motel and parked. He went inside the scant office and paid for two side by side rooms. He informed the clerk of their intentions of catching a bounty, but not her name or any details.

Inside one of the rooms, Matt hid a video camera while William watched from his computer in the other room. "You have it in a good spot," he told his partner over the portable radio. "Just make sure no one can see it."

Matt returned to the stakeout room where the crew was waiting, then handed the room key to Nick. "After a positive identification is made, we'll storm the room."

"So keep your pants on!" William jested, "We don't want to see any snakes."

"Ohh . . . I can't have a little fun with her before you guys storm the room?"

"She's a whore Nick," Dominique cautioned, "She could have something."

William lifted the receiver on the telephone and dialed a number from the newspaper for an escort service.

"Hello?" someone answered.

"Hi. I'm looking to hire a specific escort by the name of Candy Wrapper," he spoke with an odd tone while the crew held their giggles. "She comes highly recommended."

"I'm sorry, but we don't have anyone here employed by that name. However, I myself can give you excellent service."

"Thank you anyways, but I want her." He placed the receiver down onto the base, then turned toward Nick. "There's your quick training. Now it's your turn."

Nick felt a bit nervous with everyone watching and listening, however, he proceeded because he wanted a share of the bounty. He dialed a number from the newspaper and after someone answered, he asked for Candy.

"Someone else just called two minutes ago and asked for her. I don't know who she is nor does she work here."

"Oops!" He hung up quickly and cast his vision towards William. "That was the same one you called." He crossed the ad out with a pen and dialed the next classified number.

"Hello?" the receptionist answered.

"How's it going?"

"It's going well," the woman replied strangely.

"I'm lookin' for a special lady named Candy Wrapper. Am I calling the right number?"

"If it were last week, you would be. We had to let her go a few days back. May I ask who's calling?"

"Just a client."

"If you're needing an escort, I do have other girls."

"No. Candy's a favorite."

"Okay then," she replied, "If you change your mind, call us back. Bye."

"Wait!" Nick begged, "Would you be able to give me her phone number or an address?"

"I'm not suppose to . . . unless you're a detective or FBI?"

"I am," he replied, hoping for a lead. "I'm a bounty hunter."

William and Matt glared at him.

Nick wrote down an address and cell phone number, however, the address was the apartment they were just at. He ended the call with a thank you, then after comparing cell phone numbers, he dialed Candy's new number.

"Hello?" a loud voice came through.

"Candy! How's it going?"

"Who is this?" she demanded.

"Ricky B. Remember me?" He began his undertaking.

"No I don't."

"We met at the Specials Club last month. You gave me your number and said if I needed any favors—to give you a jingle."

"I've never been at the Specials Club."

"No? Maybe it was another club." Instead of hearing a reply, he heard the connection go quiet. He listened. "Candy?" He set the receiver down onto the base.

"Call her back," William urged, "But this time, try to find out where she's at now."

Nick lifted the handset, dialed from the base, and let it ring.

She answered again.

"Don't be hanging up on Ricky B. Let's hookup Sweetheart. I have a motel room and I'm ready to party!"

"I don't know you."

"But that's why we should get together. Get to know each other and you could earn a little money on the side."

"You could be a cop."

"Cops don't call you on the phone," he indicated, "They're hanging out on the streets trying to bust people."

"True . . . but I still can't trust you yet." She flipped the lid, closing her cell phone.

"Damn it!" He cast his attention to William after hanging up. "Stupid girl."

William gave thought to the situation for a moment, then used his cell phone to call her. He hadn't expected her to answer, but was glad she did. "Candy?"

"Maybe. Who is this?" she asked with a saucy tongue.

His face grew a scowl. "This will be your worst nightmare if you don't turn yourself in or tell me where you're at right now!" he vented.

"I don't have to tell you shit!" she replied.

"You quit calling Swade so he's revoking your bond. You need to come into his office and take care of this matter."

She flipped the lid on her phone, ending the call.

William turned to his team. "She did it again," he said as he closed his cell phone. "I heard familiar noises in the background—speedboats. I bet she's downtown close to the lake."

"Let's go!" Matt suggested. "We'll split up and look until we find her."

"And that's plan C," William stated.

"So we're just gonna waste these motel rooms?" Dominique asked.

"They'll be a tax write off."

They left the motel room determined to catch her. They advanced to their vehicles and drove five or six blocks. William parked alongside the curb on Sherman Avenue while Matt continued on toward Coeur d'Alene Lake on River Road. He let Dominique out so she could walk the beach. "If you spot her, radio for backup before you approach her," he advised, then drove ahead and spied from the park.

William and Nick stepped out of their truck and looked about the area before splitting into two different directions. William radioed his position to Matt and Dominique and in return, received their whereabouts report.

Nick wandered upon the sidewalk near the restaurants, between people and alongside the outdoor seating. He walked three blocks, crossed Sherman Avenue, then headed south toward the resort. He saw a lady with her arm in a sling. His heart thumped as he radioed to his crew. He hurried her way for a better view of her face.

William halted in his steps, turned and hustled in Nick's direction to assist him.

"False alarm," Nick soon reported as he went on his way.

William flipped up the lid on his cell phone and dialed Candy's number. While he let it ring, he listened for the ringing within the crowd. Maybe she was near, he had hoped. He heard nothing and she didn't answer her phone.

The next block and Nick spotted a woman who was wearing a cast. He became anxious again. If he could be the one to catch her, he thought, then he could boast of it. He walked closer wanting to identify her before calling it in. She was viewing the screen on her phone. While he stepped around a group of people, he saw that she noticed his stare. "It is her!" he mumbled to himself.

Candy turned and dashed away.

Nick took off after her. As he pursued her upon the sidewalk near Front and Second Streets, he announced his chase over the radio. He ran northwest between tourists, sometimes bumping into them. He sprang around a large potted plant, then hurtled a bench, nearly tripping.

William quickly bounced his way up Sherman Avenue. The traffic moved steadily; he stretched his neck upward trying to see ahead.

Candy gyrated her head around to peek at the distance she had gained, then hastened across a spread of grass.

Nick gasped for air as he continued dodging people, bushes, or fire hydrants. He advanced onto the lawn, nearing her.

The fugitive came to the busy Avenue and dashed toward the intersection. As she approached the crosswalk, she was startled by William who shouted out her name from beyond the other side of the street. Not having enough time to stop, she stepped out onto the blacktop. In an instant, with few pedestrians waiting to cross, a freight truck whizzed by and hit her. Her body rolled down the street. The crowd ohhed in horror as the diesel slowed and stopped.

William crossed the Avenue carefully and got to her just as Nick did.

Nick gaped at her, then at William, "I think she's dead."

He was on his cell phone with nine one one.

CHAPTER EIGHTEEN

Secrets

"Did you like it?" Critter whispered through the night into Nathan's ear as they lay together on the back seat of the stolen car. She had one leg resting atop of his.

Nathan had just caught his breath when he answered her in a low voice, "I liked it very much." He kissed her lips.

"You were my first."

"Are you sure? You were pretty good!" he offered as though he had experience himself.

"Yes I'm sure . . ." She paused. "Nathan—Do you love me?"

His arm was touching her bare breast. He thought about the hard nipple and gently rubbed it to avoid her question, but then he forced a yes.

After daybreak, Nathan awoke alone on the seat, whereby, Critter slept on the front seat. He sat up and peeked over the seat at his woman. "We should hit the road," he said when he saw that she opened her eyes.

"And stop somewhere for breakfast," she added, "I'm starving!"

Nathan looked out the window and observed the semi trucks he had parked by during the night. He noted the truck stop cafe over yonder as well as the gas pumps. He made sure they were dressed, then he hopped into the driver's seat and drove toward the eatery.

The twins were traveling on Highway 12 westward through the Gifford Pinchot National Forest near White Pass when Luke discovered the temperature needle was approaching the red section. "Damn it Reddy!" he stressed, "The engine is hot." They heard a hissing sound coming from underneath the hood and steam began to arise through the cracks of the frame. Luke slowed as he steered his truck to the side of the highway, then stopped. He cut the engine.

Reddy opened his door, stepped to the ground and walked to the front of the vehicle where he lifted the hood.

The traffic sped by. The sun was already very warm for the day, making the truck's metal hot to the touch even though they were amongst the tall Cottonwood and Pine trees. Small breezes were blowing in just enough to cool their damp foreheads, then they would start sweating again.

Luke joined his brother under the hood and hunted for the problem. He cast his vision downward at the radiator in through the small gap. He observed puffs of steam arising from the nether end so he dropped to his knees, then to his rear and down to his side. He scooted forward until his view was upon the underside of the radiator where he inspected and noted the wet hose. "The hose has a slit in it," he piped up to his brother as he dabbed the hole with a small rock.

Reddy stepped aside.

Luke stood to his feet and looked at his twin. "I'll duct tape it." He advanced to the bed of his truck, opened his tool chest, and took hold of the strong adhesive.

Reddy lit a cigarette. "Aren't you gonna let the engine cool first?"

"That'll take forever in this heat." His hairline was damp from sweat.

"It needs to cool down so we can check the water level in the radiator," he stressed.

"I know what I'm doing . . . unlike you."

"What's that suppose to mean?" he snapped.

Luke paused. "We wouldn't even be in this mess of having to go fetch Critter if it weren't for you bringing Nathan to our house."

"That's not even relevant to this situation," he roared, "You're just mad at the hose. Critter was talking about going to Grandma's two months ago and she conned Nathan into taking her."

"And the mystery to all this is solved!" Luke blurted and turned away. He stepped to the hood and looked down the small gap to see that the steam had ceased.

Reddy approached the front of the truck wearing a glove and placed it atop of the radiator cap. "Okay Luke, you don't care if it's cooled or not so I'll check it." He twisted the lid with caution, anticipating a spray of water.

After things cooled down, Luke wrapped duct tape around the hose, sealing the slit while Reddy added water to the radiator.

"We're lucky I bought this water for us to drink or we'd be stranded," Reddy claimed.

Luke agreed.

Reddy threw the empty water container into the bed of the truck and as he returned to the cab, he licked his dry lips. "I'm already thirsty, I should of saved myself a drink."

Nathan and Critter were full when they exited the cafe. "That was some good steak and eggs they served!" Nathan remarked as he rubbed his stomach.

As they walked back to their stolen car, they held hands, occasionally giving each other shy smiles.

"I have another condom," Critter blurted.

Nathan raised his brows. Feeling somewhat guilty for his previous sin, he replied, "We'd better just concentrate on getting you to your grandmother's house."

They sat onto the seats in the car and Nathan drove to the gas pumps. He turned off the engine and stepped out.

Critter eyed the Washington map while her beau pumped the gasoline, filling the tank. She soon stuck her head out the window. "You wanna take Highway 12 or head for 84?"

"Which way is the fastest?"

"Probably Highway 84 because Highway 12 goes through the forest and there's a large mountain called White Pass . . . Although Highway 12 would be a prettier drive."

The town's noon bell was ringing when Matt joined Rainy on the back porch. "So how's Aunt Penny doing?" he asked as he sat onto the swing next to her. "I heard you talking to her on the phone."

"She's been sick these past few days. She's trying to rest and stay healthy cuz she only has two weeks until she retires." There was a pause, then she sighed.

"You miss her, huh?"

"Yea."

"You wish you were there to take care of her?"

She spoke another yes.

He smiled at her. "Go pack your bags then!"

"Oh Uncle Matt. That's great! Thank you." She gave him a quick hug, then as she arose to her feet, her husband stepped out onto the porch. "Adam! Uncle Matt's buying me a round trip ticket to Phoenix!"

"What about your job?"

"It'll be okay with them," she replied as she dashed into the house.

Adam advanced toward Matt, but didn't sit on the swing next to him. Instead, he sat on a nearby lawn chair and watched him light a joint. They were both turned away from the exterior wall of the house, away from the back door, and away from the windows. Matt passed the marijuana stick to Adam. As he inhaled a toke, he listened to his uncle-in-law brag of recent acts.

"Yea . . . I had a good ole time in Phoenix when I went down there to find Rainy. I went to that strip club called Blondes on Broadway. I tell ya . . ." He paused. "There's some nice ass in that place."

"I've never been there. Rainy would kill me if I did."

Dominique was fixing clean sheets onto Ian's bed. Through the open window, she heard her husband's lustful words and her heart sank.

"Yea, if I had the chance to do it with someone hot and get away with it," Matt continued, "I would."

"Why?" Adam carried confusion upon his face. "Aunt Dominique seems to be hot enough for a thirty-six year old."

"You've only seen her with her clothes on."

Dominique sat slowly onto the foot of Ian's unmade bed. Her throat went dry and her gut ached. How much more pain could she take? she asked herself, thinking about her missing son, then returning her thoughts in on Matt's unfaithful words. Part of her couldn't believe what she was hearing. What was she going to do? Her eyes suddenly gave way to many tears.

"I'd better go see if Rainybow needs my help." Adam took one last hit off the joint before heading into the house.

While in a stupor, Dominique stood to her feet and wandered out of Ian's bedroom. She stepped across the hallway towards her own bedroom, then entered. She closed the door behind her and advanced to the bed.

She sat on her part of the mattress and recalled the hurtful or uncertain acts that Matt may or may not have done. She brought to mind his lies and sneaking about. Why did he put his wedding ring in his jeans pocket while he was out drinking at the bar? Was he trying to score with another chick? She bowed her head because she knew in her heart he was.

She looked back at the day when she peeked into the window at him and he was skimming through a dirty magazine. He hid it before she reached the door, then he denied it; said he was playing a Gameboy.

Next, she pictured from Matt's description, the stripper flaunting her open snatch close to his face. Dominique felt anger as she took in a deep breath and exhaled it. Most of the muscles in her body were tense. "It ain't right!" she rebuked as she stood to her feet. "It's unfair to me! Why should I put up with his lies, his unfaithful heart? That ain't love!" She stepped to their bureau and tore open Matt's top drawer. She grabbed his socks and underwear and flung them toward the center of the room. She did the same to the rest of his clothes before stepping to his scant entertainment center where she yanked his game system from its place, then she frisbeed his games onto the walls.

Matt heard the commotion and after he opened the door, he saw his clothes strewn about the floor, as well as his damaged goods. "Oh damn!" he mumbled.

Dominique cast her teary eyes at him and screamed. "I hate you!" Her petite bodice was quivering. She had her lips pressed tightly together as she glared at him.

"I don't want to argue . . ." he remarked.

"Of course you don't—you just want me to shut up and act as if nothing is going on!"

"Nothing is going on."

"Ha! Says you. Shall I go get another knife so you can stab me in the heart again or maybe you'd rather just twist it in deeper?" she vented. Her breathing was rapid as she stood idle, waiting for his reply.

He was silent.

"I'm tired." She let more of her words loose. "I'm tired of being hurt by you. The drinking, the deceit . . ." She looked at him. "I heard what you told Adam."

He stared at her for a moment. "When?"

"Duh?" She lifted and aimed her arm with a point of her finger towards the back porch.

"Dominique—If God didn't want women to be looked at, He wouldn't of made them beautiful."

"What a dick you are!" she remarked in haste, "You're not even sorry."

"I didn't do anything with her," he claimed.

"You're married to me!" she raised her voice, "Your vows say to be faithful to me—that includes your heart." She took in a deep breath. "God says in the Bible to not look upon a strange woman and when you do that Matt, it disrespects me, like I don't even matter."

Matt shook his head. He just wanted to turn himself around, walk out of their bedroom, and have everything be okay.

Dominique sat on her restoration sofa and eyed the mess amongst the floor. Her gut ached. "You don't love me," she spoke calmer, but still carried a serious tone, "You don't like to be sweet to me anymore. You don't give me flowers or talk dirty to me. You don't hold me at night time anymore. You don't really care about my feelings."

"Dominique?" he pleaded, but his emotions were dull. "I do love you."

"No . . . You want someone younger so I'm setting you free. I want you to leave."

"Damn it! We're getting hot again," Luke informed his brother as he glanced down at the temperature gauge.

Reddy leaned over and viewed the panel.

Luke drove another mile until he reached the top of White Pass where he noted signs for a gas station with a souvenir shop and a motel. "Doesn't look like there's a repair shop up here," he spoke as he entered the parking lot. He looked at the temperature needle again and it was now in the red. He parked at the far side of the plat and cut the engine.

Both stepped out of the truck and when they lifted the hood, steam billowed up from the bottom of the radiator and water was spraying downward onto the ground.

"Great!" Reddy spoke with sarcasm. "We'll have to look at it when it cools down."

Some ten minutes later, Luke and Reddy came out of the gas station, one eating a piece of jerky, the other a candy bar. As they neared the old white truck, they saw that the pavement underneath their vehicle now had a puddle of water and coolant mixed. They also noted the steam and hissing had quit.

Luke knelt and positioned himself to where he could examine the radiator and take a peek at his tape job on the hose. "The duct tape is still holding." He inspected the device and saw a crack where all the water had drained from. "Damn it! We need a new radiator." He withdrew himself from under the truck and cast his sights on Reddy. "I wonder if Nathan did this?"

Reddy then knelt and took a quick look at the cracked radiator. "If we mix tire sealant with some sand it will form a blockage."

"And where are you going to get this sand?" Luke smirked.

Reddy sat up onto his rear and spied the area with much thought. "Well . . . definitely not up here on the pass. "It's all dirt."

"I have Pa's visa card in case of an emergency. I'll go find a pay phone and call a tow truck from the nearest town to come get us."

"Where's your cell phone?"

"It's dead."

Within the blue sky, the moon was already visible as the day was coming to a close. After waiting six hours for the tow truck driver to show up and tow them into town, the twins were finally arriving in Packwood.

The driver turned from the main highway and drove to his repair shop. After parking, he unhooked his customer's defective truck from the tow bar. "I'll get to replacing your radiator first thing in the morning," he told them, "There's a motel just a block up the street." He pointed toward the city's center.

Luke and Reddy shifted themselves around and headed in the direction the man suggested and soon came upon a dance club.

"You know what I'm thinking Bro," Luke spoke to him with a grin.

CHAPTER NINETEEN

Terror At Grandma's House

Nathan and Critter were both in need of a shower and their stomachs were again rumbling when they arrived into Rainier. Nathan drove the way Critter was directing; over a huge steel bridge and onto a large bend that went up a lofty land mass. At the top of the hill, he exited onto a side road and soon turned again onto a dirt lane.

"There's Grandma's house!" Critter pointed out.

Nathan steered the car into the driveway, parked, then cut the engine.

"I don't see my grandma's car anywhere," she remarked with concern.

"She's probably out running errands. How old is she?"

"I think she's sixty."

They exited the stolen car. Critter grabbed her pillow while Nathan carried her two bags. She stopped at the large bay window and peeked in. She saw her grandmother's furniture as well as her many antique trinkets and photographs. Critter quit spying and continued on toward the anterior door of the house, then she tested the knob. "We need to find a key," she said to Nathan as she cast her eyes upon him.

He looked underneath a flower pot and it was there. "How lucky is that?" He keyed the lock and they entered in.

"Grandma?" Critter called out.

Nathan dropped the luggage onto the hardwood floor and closed the door.

Critter stepped through the hall into the kitchen.

Nathan circled his sights about the room and sniffed. "Pew! It smells like a grandma's house," he remarked with the raise of his voice. He then spotted a telephone so he quickly stepped to it and lifted the receiver. There was no dial tone.

Critter returned to the living room and observed him setting the phone down. She didn't want him calling anyone because she wanted him all to herself; No Pa, no Luke and Reddy, and now no Grandma. "She's not here," she said as she advanced to him.

He looked at her. "Where could she be?"

"Probably on one of her trips." The room was dim. She stepped to the entryway and flipped the light switch upward. "We should park the car in the garage, then we can take our showers and eat."

The next morning, Critter awoke first. She used the restroom and gargled with her grandmother's mouthwash. She didn't remember going to bed after dinner last night because she was so tired. She washed her hands and returned to her grandmother's bedroom where she had slept alone.

Wearing only a large t-shirt for a nightgown, she advanced to the door and after opening it, she walked out to the hall. She went to the guest bedroom and peeked in. Nathan was lying face up gazing at the ceiling. She pushed the door open a few inches and poked her head in.

"Hey?" he greeted when the squeak of the door alerted him to her standing in that place. He noticed her skimpy outfit.

"Can I come in?"

He felt nervous, but told her hell yea.

She sat on the bed next to him. "You'll stay here with me won't you? I don't want to be here by myself." She expressed a sad face for him to see, one he couldn't resist.

"Yea, I suppose, but how can you get a hold of your grandma?"

"I can't."

He thought on that. "How long had your grandma's longest trip been?"

"About a month I guess."

"So if she left yesterday, you'd want me to stay here a month?"

"Uh-hu." She curved a half grin.

"What about your Pa?" He really meant Luke and Reddy.

"I don't care right now. I just like it with me and you."

He didn't say a word. He stared at her as he leaned backwards onto his pillow and the headboard. He had his arms bent upward with his hands underneath the back of his head.

She sensed his uncertainty. "I'll make your stay worth it." She arose to a stand and began swaying her hips to and fro.

He gave her a big grin.

She turned herself around, bent over and touched her ankle bracelet.

"Oh damn Critter!" he blurted when he saw that she wasn't wearing any underwear. He threw his blanket aside and leaped towards her.

Detective Amy was at her desk working on her computer with another case when she received a phone call from the credit card company telling her that Luke Meyer's card had been used last night and again this morning. "Packwood, Washington huh?" she repeated back to the receptionist.

She quickly finished what she was working on, then left her station to go see Detective Morris. She stopped at his cubicle and popped her head in through the entryway. "We're going on a trip!"

He knew to grab his overnight bag.

Nathan stood in front of the bay window and scanned the outdoors. He observed the tree branches bending from the wind, then he gazed upwards at the dark clouds that were moving in from the far distance. He inhaled a large breath through his nostrils. "I can smell the rain from here!" he murmured to himself.

He was now bored. He had already toured Grandma's large house looking for any communication device; a computer or maybe even a cell phone that had a few minutes left on it. He cast his vision about the grassy fields and down the scant roadway where he observed a police vehicle nearing their vicinity. "Critter?" he called out with a turn of his head, then stooped below the window sill. "I think we have company."

Critter entered the dim lighted living room and saw Nathan on the floor. She dropped and crawled to the window where she took a peek.

"I can't remember if I locked the door!" Nathan exclaimed even though he wouldn't mind being seen and questioned so he could go home, however, Critter wanted him to stay.

She scampered to the door and checked the knob, then motioned with her hand for him to follow her.

He went to her and they stood against the wall just past the foyer and listened.

The officers knocked.

Nathan heard the pounding of Critter's heart. "Don't be scared," he whispered.

"What if they come in?"

"They won't. I still have the key in my pocket."

"But what if they kick the door in?"

"They don't have any reason to."

After the two cops searched the outside of the property and spied in through a few windows, they reported the house to be empty, then left.

Nathan and Critter watched the patrol car as it faded down the road.

"You have any more of that weed?" he asked her.

"I have another joint in my bag. I'll get it after we eat our lunch."

He followed her into the kitchen.

She stepped to the oven and opened the door. "I had this baking for us." She lifted and carried a pan containing two large chicken pot pies.

"Smells good." He grabbed the plates, forks, and soft drinks, then walked behind her.

She left the kitchen. She tread the staircase and advanced through the hallway, then entered a bedroom and set the hot pan onto the bureau. She stepped into the closet and opened a small door. "It's our old playhouse."

"Awesome!" he responded as he neared. "You have all kinds of secret little places to go to."

She smiled at him.

He watched as she ducked and entered the unseen enclosure. He soon heard a click and the light came on. He took hold of the food and joined her in her playhouse for an indoor picnic.

Forty-five minutes later and their stomachs were full, however, they were now thirsty from getting high. Critter leaned in and gave Nathan a kiss. "I'll go get us another drink."

"Just get me cold water."

She arose to her feet and stepped out into the dark bedroom. She glanced out the window and noted some fast moving clouds breezing by the moon, then she advanced into the gloomy unlit hallway.

When she came to the bottom of the staircase, she saw light emitting from the kitchen. "I thought I switched that light off." She turned and headed into the light. When she entered the kitchen, she was stopped by sudden fear. "Oh my gosh! What are you guys doing here?"

Nathan stepped out of the errie closet and stretched his back, then his arms and legs. He had remembered the fireworks he'd found earlier and wanted to fire one up. With his t-shirt, he wiped a small amount of sweat from his brow. He listened to the wind blow the branches across the roof, but he wouldn't let that stop him from a little fun. He exited the bedroom, went through the dark hallway, and down the staircase. He heard a muffled scream coming from the kitchen so he tiptoed forward for a better listen.

"Where is he?" Reddy thundered at his sister.

"He's not here!" she claimed, "He dropped me off and left."

"Oh he's here. There's a strange car in the garage." He grabbed her arm.

"That's grandma's car. It was here when we got here."

"Sure it was." Luke and Reddy forced her down onto a chair and held her.

"What are you going to do to him?" she yelled.

"We have to silence him, then you're going back home to Pa."

Nathan was shocked to hear them taping and gagging their own sister. "Screw this," he said to himself as he turned and crept away. "I'm outta here!" He stepped up his pace through the large living room and when he came upon the foyer, he heard Reddy's command to Luke.

"Let's go find his ass!"

He didn't know if he had time to get to the front door and exit the house so without further thought, he slipped into the nearest door.

He had the basement door almost closed when he detected heavy footsteps at close range, then they faded up the stairwell. He knew Luke and Reddy would find where he and critter just had dinner, as well as where he slept last night. His mind flashed through many thoughts. He realized they were there to kill him. His heart raced. "Please don't let them kill me God." He lifted his face skyward. He knew he needed a plan; a McGyver plan that would allow him to capture Luke and Reddy, or worse a self defense killing.

As he stood on the top step in the dark, he saw a flash of lightening through the basement window, followed by the roar of thunder. He switched the light on and scanned the surroundings once again. He saw a flashlight on the shelf and remembered seeing it this morning. He returned his hand to the switch and turned the light off, then flicked his lighter so he could unscrew the warm bulb.

Nathan descended the steps and grabbed the flashlight. He aimed the beam onto the window so he could open it. The breeze blew the musty curtain aside and he could smell the oncoming storm in the air. He eyed the width of the window and thought of going out, but didn't think he'd fit.

Next he hastened to a small rope that was hanging on the wall and cast it down to the floor. He advanced to the far corner of the basement and removed his stash of rockets from the cabinet. "These must have been her Grandpa's rockets," he entertained as he returned to the bottom of the staircase, just out of sight of the doorway, and knelt. He was going to blast em' when they opened the door and tie them up.

"Where's that punk?" Reddy thundered as he searched the bedrooms and playhouse.

Luke spied the empty bathroom, then joined Reddy in the hallway. He saw the rage in his brother's face and seized onto his arm. "Wait! Why don't we just take Critter and go home?" He panted for air as he waited for a reply.

"He's made a fool of me," he fumed, "I'm going to kill him!"

"How?"

Reddy spoke stern. "I guess I'll have to bash him on the head, then dump his body alongside the highway."

"You sure that's what you want to do?" Luke begged as he let go of his arm.

Reddy gave his brother an icy stare, then turned and hurried down the stairwell.

Luke followed him down the staircase.

Reddy hunted for Nathan on the main floor, the far side of the large house.

Luke approached and cracked open the basement door for a peek inside. He noted the darkness and he could hear the storm through the open window. He widened the door, stepped onto the first step, and attempted three times to switch the light on. After no glow of the light, he lifted his hand to the bulb.

Nathan's heart pounded and his hands shook as he flicked his lighter to ignite the fuse. He quickly scooted a foot and pointed the rocket at Luke. The missile thrust forward, making contact. The tip entered and became embedded into his lower back and the underside of the rocket was still throwing sparks.

"Oh fuck!!" Luke expelled as he stumbled in pain; his leg giving out and he dropped. The rocket came out and landed on one of the steps.

Nathan watched in awe as Luke came rolling and tumbling down the steps. With the thudding, he knew Reddy would be near. He clutched onto the rope and as soon as Luke hit the cement flooring, he jumped on him. Using the glow from the upstairs light, he wrapped the thin rope around Luke's wrists, making a quick knot. He was out cold.

Nathan took hold of a small wooden oar and stepped warily up the steps, expecting Reddy to appear any time. He opened his mouth for better breathing. He could feel his heart thumping even harder than before; Reddy isn't going to be as easy to take down as Luke, he told himself.

Critter kept silent when her brothers had neglected to actually tape her to the chair. After they had stormed out of the kitchen, she stood to her feet and hopped across the room to get at her Grandmother's knife set.

With her wrists taped together, she grabbed onto a large chopping knife and carefully sat onto the floor. She sliced the tape from her ankles, then brought her feet in close toward her and placed the blade right side up between her heels. She positioned her bound wrists atop of the blade's edge and slowly slid the tape back and forth until it split.

Nathan touched his outer pocket to make sure he still carried the car key before arriving to the top of the staircase. His new plan was to get to the garage as fast as he could and speed away in his stolen car.

He peeked out the basement door and thinking it was clear, he stepped out. He advanced into the foyer and after taking a few steps, he heard a creaking sound behind him so he turned and was instantly struck by a fist. Him and his oar went backwards; he bounced off the wall and the oar landed on the floor. He knew he should of ducked. He sprang forward with a hard knuckle of his own for Reddy.

Reddy's head spun, followed by his torso. He dropped to the floor, but rolled away before Nathan could whack him with a nearby lamp. The electrical device broke when it came into contact with the hardwood floor and he tossed it aside.

Reddy was in the act of standing when Nathan lunged at him causing both to give way to the maple flooring. As they wrestled around, fists were being swung into each other's guts or faces until Nathan was able to wrap his arm around Reddy's neck. He used all of his strength to enforce the choke hold. "You're not a good fighter, are you?" he taunted, adrenaline pumping.

The lightening struck the ground outside and the thunder vibrated the house. The wind blew its power through the trees causing the limbs to scrape against the house.

Critter came running into the gloom filled room and saw the brawling. "Stop it!" she cried out as she leaped onto Nathan's back. "You're hurting my brother!"

"He wants to kill me!" he roared in response to her command while he continued to hold his arms tightly around Reddy's neck as though he was about to win a match.

"No he doesn't . . ." she blurted, "He's not like that."

"It's me or them Critter. Choose a side!" He had to release his grip from Reddy because of her tugs and scratches. They both went to their butts with a thud and Reddy lay motionless.

Nathan sprang to his feet while Critter crawled to her sibling. "Reddy?" she begged of him as she lovingly tapped his face with her hand.

While Critter attempted to revive her brother, Nathan panted for air, realizing her answer. He knew it was time for him to really leave. "Bye Critter."

She cast a look of shock upon him. "Don't leave me Nathan!" she pleaded, "I want you to stay."

"It wouldn't work out."

She arose to her feet and stepped to him. "We'll make it work."

"No!" he replied firmly, "I'm going home." He gently pushed her away, then turned to leave. He entered and jogged through the kitchen.

Reddy was coughing and barely moving when Critter gave chase to Nathan.

Nathan opened the door that led to the garage and advanced down the step. As he stepped toward the car, he pulled the key from his pocket, but before he could reach the handle to the car door, Critter grabbed onto his arm, causing the key to drop to the cement and bounce under the vehicle.

"Nathan—I love you!" she fussed as she tugged on him.

"Let go of me Critter." He was aching to get out of there before Reddy caught up to him. He shoved her, then cast his eyes to the ground and knelt. He reached beneath the car and felt for the key.

A desperate Critter opened the car's rear door and climbed into the back seat.

Nathan snatched up the metal device, then uplifted himself to his feet. He opened his door and leaped atop of the driver's seat. He glanced in the rear view mirror. "Get out Critter!" he ordered as he inserted the key into the ignition.

"No!"

"You stay here with your family. You're only fifteen."

"So," she replied, "We can still spend more time together before I have to go home to my Pa. In the meantime, I'll tell Luke and Reddy to leave you alone," she begged.

"You're almost as crazy as your brothers," he blurted.

"What?"

"Just get out." He looked in the mirror to see her sitting idle. Her arms were crossed and she wore a scowl upon her face. "Will you go open the garage door for me?"

"You want me to get out of the car so you can lock me out."

"If you won't get out and press the garage door button, I'll ram the door," he threatened, then started the engine.

"Go ahead!" she spoke with a daring tongue.

His heart beat fast. He shifted into reverse and when he glanced in the mirror so he could back to the wall, he saw Reddy appear at the garage entry holding his throat. His face exhibited wrath.

"Go away Reddy!" Critter shouted.

As fast as he could, Nathan backed, then moved the gear into drive and stomped on the gas pedal. The tires were spinning and smoking.

Reddy lunged for the door handle, but Critter had locked the doors. "Open the door Critter!" he roared while he banged on the window.

The car went forward, hitting, then bending the thin metal of the door as it continued through. The impact forced the door to come off its track and it lay broken.

Nathan accelerated out of the driveway onto the dirt lane. He turned his headlights on. "Whew-hu!" he howled. He was glad he made it out, however, he still had the problem of Critter sitting on the back seat.

As he neared the stop sign, he came upon a fleet of cars turning onto grandma' street, one being a police car. "Yes!" He stopped and parked his vehicle.

"No Nathan," Critter growled when she saw the police convoy.

"Bye Critter." He cut the engine and stepped out into the stormy night.

"You're a heartless jerk!" she yelled.

He advanced toward the police car.

"Hold it right there!" the cop ordered after he stepped out of his car and aimed the beam of his flashlight on the young man.

Nathan ceased from walking and presented his empty hands. "I need to tell you that I've been missing from my mom for about a month . . . I think a month and the guys who took me are in that large yellow house." He pointed in the direction of which he just came. "Their sister is in the car."

The two detectives exited their car and stepped to the young man and cop.

The officer briefed them.

"Are you Nathan Kiniky?" Detective Amy asked him.

"Yes."

She smiled. "We've been looking for you."

CHAPTER TWENTY

Encore

The morning sun radiated in through the bare window making it hard for a person to sleep. Matt tossed and turned from the glare, finally forcing himself to get up to go close the shade.

He stumbled back to the couch and flopped down. He smacked his dry lips, wanting a drink of pepsi to cover the foul taste in his mouth, but instead, he pulled the blanket over him and resumed sleeping.

The Underdog's office door opened and William entered. "Phew!" he exclaimed to himself after taking two steps in. "What died in here?" He flipped both the ceiling fan and light switch on and when he cast his eyes about the space, he observed Matt lying on the firm's sofa, snoring. He saw empty beer bottles spread out upon Matt's desk causing a surge of anger to run through his body.

Matt awoke when the lights were turned on. While his vision came into focus, he sat up.

William seated himself at his own desk and cast a fixed stare at his partner. "Rough night?"

"Yea." He thought briefly of Dominique as he yawned and stretched.

"Swade will be here in about fifteen minutes."

Matt stood to his feet and advanced to his desk where he collected the bottles and placed them in a small garbage can. He carried the container out to the alleyway and chucked them in the recycling bin, not caring if they broke.

When he returned to the office, William was on the phone with Travis, telling him to fetch Adam and come in to work.

"We'll be there in twenty minutes," he replied back to him.

"I just heard it on the scanner!" Swade exclaimed with much concern after he entered The Underdog's office and stepped toward William. "There's a mad hunt going on right now for Billy Peterson."

Matt perked up. "Billy Boobs?" he asked, but was ignored.

"He just shot a cop, then took off on foot."

William turned in his swivel chair slightly to his right and switched on their own scanner to listen, then looked at Swade.

"He's violating my bond by running."

"I hate to interfere with the police on this." William glanced at Matt.

"What about going after Steven today?" Matt posed as he cast his sights onto Swade, then back at William. "Tomorrow?"

"I would appreciate it if you went after Billy today," Swade spoke to the bounty hunters, "His bond is larger."

"What the hell—We'll be heroes if we catch him!" William boasted.

Travis and Adam arrived, each carrying a duffel bag as they entered the office. Seeing William and Matt gearing up, they headed toward the sofa to do the same.

"Hello boys!" William greeted, "We're going after Billy Boobs again."

Swade sipped on his coffee as he stood waiting.

"Our first stop, the crime scene. I want to get as close in to it as possible."

"Maybe we should be looking in the trees for him?" Travis joked.

The crew chuckled, especially Adam.

Before leaving, they heard over the scanner the report and that a shot had been fired from the officer's gun.

Her eyes dripped tears while she sprayed her rosebushes with the nozzle from the garden hose. Dominique's thoughts were back and forth between filing for divorce and Nathan's whereabouts. She quit watering and as she headed toward her empty hose, she dried her eyes. Instead of stepping into the kitchen, she sat on her porch swing and prayed.

Before long, she detected the ringing of her telephone. She presumed it to be Matt, however, she was encouraged to go answer the call because of her missing son.

In the living room, she lifted the receiver from the base and after a quick greeting, she heard only the dial tone. "Dang it!"

Detective Amy closed her cell phone. "Still no one is answering," she told her partner who was sitting next to Nathan as he napped. "I'll try again after we land."

His heart pounded with fear and his body was pumping adrenaline. The recent memory of him pulling the trigger flashed within his polluted mind as he paused alongside a concrete building and panted for air. The faint sound of sirens roared from two blocks away and the rain was now pounding down atop of his curly hair; he was getting wet fast.

Billy took a glance at his bullet wound and decided he needed to lay low. He scanned the area and saw a veterinary clinic across a large parking lot. He turned his head to quickly search for pursuers or suspecting people, saw no one, then jogged through many water puddles as he set out for the animal infirmary.

Matt wanted to let Dominique know of his dangerous and forthcoming outting, but was unsure if he should call for fear of harsh words or an argument evolving. He dialed on his cell phone her number and let it ring. When he heard her voice on the other end, he hung up.

The team arrived into Coeur d' Alene. Working from two separate vehicles, Matt followed behind William as he exited the freeway and drove north on Highway 95 to Dalton Avenue. He took a left turn, however, the road ahead had a blockade so he steered his vehicle into a detour.

The rain had decreased to sprinkles and a large rainbow could be seen across the sky.

The bounty hunters came upon a small unsaturated patch of ground to park the SUV's, then William and Matt grabbed their binoculars and exited. While standing by the hood of their truck, they put the devices to their eyes and focused in on the crime scene. The ambulance was gone; it had already raced away with the injured police officer. He saw the area to be outlined with yellow 'Do Not Cross' tape, whereas, many detectives were within the perimeter processing the scene. The patrol car remained unmoved with its driver's door open and evidence markers were placed beside the bullet shells about the pavement.

William drew his vision to the surrounding lots and buildings, then studied the layout of the nearby streets. "He may have taken off that way," he suggested to Matt as they both faced north. "I don't think he'd go home," he spoke, recalling Billy's residence to be just south of them. They withdrew the binoculars from their eyes.

"No—the cops would already have him in custody if he'd gone home," Matt answered as he fired up a cigarette.

"I want to head to the other side to start looking for possible footprints and I feel you and Travis should go see what those reporters are reporting."

"Sounds good," Matt complied as his partner turned and walked to the door of his vehicle. "Then we'll meet up with you." He cast his vision onto Travis and gestured for him to follow.

With Swade and Adam aboard, William drove the back way around the block to another side street, then parked alongside the curb.

Matt and Travis stood by the edge of the yellow tape and listened to a reporter as she spoke from under an umbrella into the microphone.

"The rain has thrown off the scent for the k-9 dog," she reported in front of the news camera. "However, law enforcement is still combing the vicinity and ask anyone who has seen Billy Peterson or suspicious activity in the Dalton area is to call the police. You can remain anonymous."

William studied the crime scene again as he stood at the edge of the street. He noted the k-9 dog as it shook the rain from its fur, then the officer directed the animal into the rear cage of his truck. William counted the evidence markers; some knocked over by the wind. He watched a forensic's detective swab what he thought to be a large droplet of blood. He lowered his binoculars and looked at Swade. "Billy's been hit!"

"So it seems," he replied as he withdrew his own portable field glasses.

They turned and after walking back to their truck, Matt and Travis drove up and parked behind them. They exited the vehicle and joined in with the team.

The bounty hunters eyed the wet ground in starting their search for Billy Boobs. Sections of the street were drying from the wind and the gusts were causing ripples in the water puddles.

When Billy Boobs came upon the hinder part of the animal clinic, he noticed a half of a cigarette was burning within a tin can outside of the building and the back door was slightly open. He peeked in through the crack and observed no employees to be in sight, but could hear them talking from a distance. He saw sleeping animals in their cages as he entered with discretion. He scanned the section and noted a possible room beyond a brown wooden door so he advanced and as he opened and stepped in, he found it to be a large broom closet. He pulled the door shut and switched on the light.

His hair and forehead were wet from both sweat and rain, but mostly from the rain. He grabbed hold of a roll of paper towel from the shelf and without unrolling it, he dabbed his brow, then rolled it upon his head. He tossed the damp roll to the corner and sat down.

His breathing had slowed, however, with every exhale his humped tongue came out of his mouth, then back in again.

Billy moved his wet sleeve up past his elbow and examined the wound on his arm more efficiently. "Ha—Just a scratch!" he murmured, then returned the hem of his sleeve to his wrist. He reached behind his back and pulled his gun out from the edge of his pants and set it on the floor.

As he sat idle in the corner listening, he heard the mewing of weak kittens from the other room. Soon he detected the presence of two employees stepping about as they tended to their work.

"Did you leave the closet light on?" he heard the female assistant ask the veterinarian as she advanced toward the closet door.

"No," he replied.

Billy kept his eyes on the underpart of the door and watched the shadow from her feet. He took hold of his gun.

The door opened just to a foot.

He raised his weapon.

Her upper arm came in and she switched off the light. She re-closed the door and returned to the cages.

Billy found himself awaking from a doze; he didn't know how long he'd been sleeping. As he sat up, he recalled his whereabouts, then focused in on the light shining in from underneath the door. He arose to his knees, went toward and switched the closet light back on. He grabbed two rolls of paper towel and pressed them vertically alongside the gap, then returned to sitting in the corner.

He drew from his pants pocket, a dollar bill and a small wad of paper in which he unfolded carefully and set on the floor. He rolled the dollar bill into a tight straw, then lifted the paper from the floor and commenced to snorting the white drug.

After twenty minutes, the closet door opened.

Caught off guard, Billy held his breath and stayed idle.

The assistant's hand and forearm appeared. She locked the door on the inside of the knob, switched the light off, then slammed the door shut. "I bet the secretary is the one who keeps forgetting to turn off the light," she scolded aloud to the doctor.

Stepping alongside the curb on a side street, the bounty hunters probed the wet ground, looking for anything significant in their hunt for Billy. They trekked north finding not one droplet of blood or muddy footprint.

Arriving at the end of the block, Travis observed a group of trees behind a building. "Come on!" He motioned to Adam with a hand gesture, turned and jogged through the alley.

Travis and Adam looked upward and while they spied within the branches, a patrol car cruised by.

William, Swade, and Matt stopped on the sidewalk and did a visual search of the area, then crossed a busy street and entered into a parking lot. The Underdogs bypassed a few buildings and soon came upon a young woman who was leaned against a brick wall, smoking a cigarette.

"Hello!" William greeted with a tilt of his head.

She eyed their distinct bounty hunting outfits as she returned the welcome. "You guys looking for someone?"

"Yes," Matt replied, "A very large and dangerous man."

"Haven't seen anyone come through here. Is that what all those sirens are about?"

William nodded.

Hearing barks from dogs a block away, the team departed and continued going north.

The vet technician gave quick thought to the odd situation of the closet light. Could he be hiding in there? she asked herself, then became concerned and afraid. She didn't want to confront the large and dangerous man herself even though she didn't know for sure if he was actually in the closet or not. She dropped her cigarette butt into the tin can and chased after the bounty hunters.

The bounty hunters wanted to see if the technician's theory held any truth to it so after seeing why the dogs were barking, they returned to the animal clinic. When they came to the rear entrance of the building, Matt stepped in and blocked William's path. "Wait! Maybe we should just let the cops get him out of that closet?"

"He's Swade's bond so that means Billy is ours for the catching," William spoke with a scowl upon his face. "It's also a matter of revenge. That Bastard shot at me too!"

Matt exhaled. "You're right. Let's go get him!" He stepped aside and let William lead. Travis brought up the rear and Adam was sent back to fetch one of the vehicles.

The three Underdogs stepped softly through the doorway of the building and saw the brown wooden door. William and Matt drew their pistols, then inched their way toward the locked closure. As they stood at the edges of the door frame, they held their breathing and listened.

Billy Boobs Peterson had switched off the light and removed the paper towel rolls from the gap at the foot of the door. He thought he'd continue to lay low throughout the night so he watched and waited and soon he saw the shadows of feet beneath the door.

Matt stepped in front of the cheap wooden door and without discussion, he lifted his leg and gave the door a kick close to the knob. It burst open. He aimed his gun, but Billy was quicker on the draw. He soared backwards.

William was flabbergasted, yet angry. He quickened his loaded pistol past the border of the doorway and exchanged fire with the criminal.

The veterinarian who was standing by the far counter ran to his office to call an ambulance. He had hoped none of his animals got in the way of the gunfire.

Travis heard the click of both Billy's weapon and William's and knew they were out of bullets. With a taser gun fixed in his hands, he dove from the rear entrance and slid on his stomach upon the linoleum floor until he reached the open doorway, then discharged the prongs and volts. "Awesome!" he spoke under his breath as he watched Billy quiver and quake.

"Aahhh . . ." Billy was roaring.

As fast as he could, William inserted his pistol into his holster and while he ran to Billy, he took hold of a pair of handcuffs from his belt. He knelt, pressing one knee onto Billy's large back.

"Get off me! Aahh . . ."

Travis sprang to his feet and raced to help subdue the three hundred pound, enraged man. He seized his own pair of handcuffs, dropped, and clutched onto the arm that William didn't have. Billy was squirming.

"Hold still!" William yelled, then with a fist, he quickly socked Billy in the chops.

"You can't hit me!" he protested with high volume as he lay face down.

"I didn't hit you—nobody saw a thing!" He punched him again—dazing him, then together, he and Travis bagged Coeur d' Alene's most wanted.

Matt lay bleeding. He held onto his chest as he listened to the takedown of Billy Boobs Peterson.

CHAPTER TWENTY-ONE

Heroes Or Criminals?

A call had just come in from Travis. Dominique paced the floor as she thought about getting in her car and driving to the Coeur d' Alene hospital. Only an hour ago she was on the telephone talking to her divorce lawyer.

Ian stepped into the room with his Pokemon cards, sat on the couch, and watched his mom.

The telephone rang again. Dominique answered the call right away.

"Hi Dominique-" Detective Amy greeted, "I have a big surprise for you!"

Her heart began to pound with anticipation. She could hear the excitement in the woman's voice.

"We've just landed in Spokane! We found your son in . . ."

Dominique fell to her knees; she went numb. Barely able to speak, she asked if Nathan was okay.

Hearing his brother's name, Ian sprang from the couch and rushed to stand beside his mom.

"You can ask him yourself," the detective replied, then handed her cellular phone to Nathan.

"Hi Mom," he spoke softly.

Her voice trembled when she spoke, "Nathan—" Tears rolled down her cheeks. "I knew you were alive. Where did you go?"

Nathan became teary eyed so he turned away from the detectives as he talked to his mom.

After William and Adam surrendered Billy Boobs Peterson to the county jail, they drove to the hospital. They parked next to their other company vehicle, climbed out, and stepped to the hind part of both rigs.

Travis had lifted and was standing under the hatch inspecting Matt's bullet proof vest. He was touching the two bullet imprints with his thumbs. "He's still in the emergency room," he told his comrades as he cast his eyes on them. "I don't know his condition, but the paramedics said he was conscious and he was speaking in the ambulance."

"Where's Swade?" William asked.

"I think he's inside. He was talking on his phone to someone."

"Let's get inside and see how Matt's doing. Did you call your mom?"

"Yea."

They locked the SUV's, then still attired in their navy blue t-shirts that read The Underdogs Bounty Team, they headed toward the medical facility. When they neared the entrance doors, two reporters and their cameramen approached them.

"Are you the bounty hunters who captured Billy Peterson?" one queried as they rushed to get in their faces.

"Sure was!" Travis boasted into the microphone as he looked at the camera.

"Can you tell us how you took him down?"

William butted in. "No—it's all in the police report. We need to get inside." He nudged Travis and Adam toward the automatic doors. They entered the building and soon found Swade sitting within the waiting room.

Before anyone could say a word, a nurse advanced in through another door and spoke as she stepped to the group. "You can see Matt Jax now, but only for five minutes."

"Why only five minutes?" Travis asked.

"He's going into surgery."

Just when Travis and William turned to follow the medical personnel, Rainy hastened in. "They found Nathan! The detectives are bringing him home right now."

Travis cast his sights at William. "I'm going home."

Adam left with Rainy while Swade waited for William to visit Matt.

William proceeded alone down the corridor to Matt's bedside behind the curtain. He observed the usual medical equipment and health care products within the ward. He saw that Matt wore an IV as well as temporary gauze about his armpit and shoulder. He cleared his throat to get his partner's attention.

Matt opened his eyes.

"Hey partner?" he spoke low.

"Bullet went straight through my shoulder." He was groggy from the medication. "They said I be okay though." He turned his head slightly away as he closed his eyes.

William leaned in close to his ear. "I'm sorry I had to rush out of the vet clinic with Billy, but I had to before the fuzz arrived."

"Did anyone else get hurt?" His mind was blurred, not caring too much about William's apology right now.

"No—you're the only one. I'm a terrible shot."

Back at the estate, Dominique and Ian waited out by the gate for Nathan to arrive and soon enough, the government issued car neared.

Nathan had his head out the rear side window. "Mom!" he shouted to her.

It took her breath away. She couldn't believe her eyes.

Before the engine was cut, Nathan had the door open and he was leaping out. The detectives were merry.

Ian jumped up and down several times while he and his mom advanced. She began to laugh with joy as she placed a hand over her mouth. She stepped forward, watching Nathan. They met half way in the driveway where she embraced her long lost son.

Ian moved in and wrapped his arms around his brother's waist.

They parted. Dominique fixed her shaky hands onto his cheeks. "How are you?" She gazed into his familiar face with her watery eyes.

"I'm glad to be home," he replied.

The two detectives exited their vehicle and informed Dominique that Luke and Reddy were in custody and they would be transported back to Shoshone County to face charges; the girl would most likely be released to her father.

Another vehicle pulled up alongside the gate. Travis exited his truck and hastened to the group; he recognized the two detectives. "Hey Bro—It's good to see you." He gave him a manlike hug.

After the brief reunion, Dominique and her sons walked the sidewalk to the house.

"I want to go see my room." Nathan cast his big brown eyes to his mom. "Did you keep my stuff?"

She smiled. "Of course I kept your stuff."

Travis and Ian followed Nathan upstairs while their mother fired up the charcoal grill and prepared the hamburgers.

Nathan scanned his bedroom to find everything the same, then he leaned in close to Travis' ear and spoke, "I got laid twice."

"Critter?"

Adam and Rainy Bow arrived home from the hospital and Nick swung by for a visit. They joined the family in the backyard for the special occasion.

"So this is Nathan?" Adam asked Dominique in a comical manner as he and Rainy stepped close. He extended his hand to Nathan. "Nice to meet you."

Nathan shook his hand.

Dominique introduced them to her son, then listened to Rainy as she told her that she and Adam would be moving out of her house tomorrow, then she would be flying to Arizona.

They slept in late. When Dominique emerged from her bedroom, she heard voices coming from the living room. One in particular was Nathan and Ian's paternal grandmother so she directed herself into the kitchen. She didn't care much to talk to her ex mother-in-law.

She exited quietly through the rear door of the house and stepped to the porch. She lit a cigarette and in a short while, Ian found her sitting on the swing.

"I brought you the newspaper."

"Thank you Baby Zebra."

He sat next to her.

"I take it your grandma left?" she asked.

"Yea."

Dominique unrolled the paper and beheld the headlines. "Heroes or criminals?" Her blue eyes widened as she began to read the article about Matt and William. She wondered if they would be in trouble with the law for interfering and if Matt's bounty hunting business is in jeopardy?

She set the newspaper on the deck and gazed upward.

Ian could see she was lost in thought. "Are you thinking about Matt?" he asked.

"Yea, but I don't want to be."

"Are you going to the hospital to see him?"

"No—I'm still too angry at him."

"I don't want to see him no more either. He's a drunk." He rested his head against her arm. "I'll pray for us."

"I'll pray for us too." She patted the top of his noggin with her hand.

Nathan joined his mom and younger brother on the porch. He sat onto a lawn chair and commented on the warm breeze.

"It's going to be a hot day," Ian added to the conversation.

"And I don't have to do any yard work!" Nathan exclaimed, then briefed his mom on the terrific job he'd done making his kidnapper's back yard look like the Garden of Eden.

After other talk, she asked him what he wanted to do today?

"Well, Sandy's coming over. We were gonna go up to the Glen for a little while."

"Don't get into any strangers cars!" Her reaction was swift and firm.

He grinned.

Ian saw Nathan's smirk. "It ain't funny Nathan! I thought you were dead."

"Mom didn't think I was dead," he replied.

Dominique stood to her feet. "I'm going back into the house. Don't stay gone all day." She looked at Nathan. "Maybe we'll go shopping."

Nathan arose and moved to sit beside Ian on the swing. They engaged in small talk as they faced the back yard and beyond.

A movement in the lush acreage caught Ian's eye. "Did you see that?" he asked Nathan as he leaned aside and watched. He soon saw what he thought to be his neighbor Damian darting out from behind a pine tree and rushing to hide behind another.

"What's that little sneak doing?" Nathan wondered.

"I don't know," Ian replied, "but I'm not scared this time cuz you're here."

"Why would you be scared? He's only a little bigger than you."

"He had a knife . . ."

"So," he interrupted, "Kick him in the balls—he'll go down."

Ian snickered as he squeezed his hands together and gritted his teeth.

They again focused in on the plot of land and observed Damian running and somewhat diving behind a bush.

"He's got his camouflage clothes on and he's got something under his arm!" Ian exclaimed, then with an idea, he smiled and ran into the house. He dashed up the stairwell to Nathan's bedroom and grabbed hold of his BB gun. He held it next to his body and as he came down the staircase, he walked with caution, hoping his mother didn't see him.

Once outside, he fixed his vision on the bush where he last saw Damian.

"He crawled over to that large rock," Nathan informed him.

Ian dashed away.

"I want my BB gun back in five minutes!" he blurted out, then after quick thought, he decided to join him in his surprise attack, so he rushed to catch up.

At the far end of the yard, they came upon and circled about the garage. They stopped at the building's end and Ian poked his head past the edge to take a peek. Before he could pull back, a foam bullet came soaring and stuck onto his forehead.

"Nice shot!" Nathan was amazed with Damian's aim as he reached out and yanked the toy device from his brother's face.

Ian giggled. "He's not going to hurt me. He just wants to play."

"Even so, you still gonna take that crap from him?" He urged him to take immediate action.

Ian thought about the knife as he pumped the BB gun seven times. He spied from the edge of the garage and waited for Damian to show himself. It wasn't too long a time until his pal was on the move again. He quickly took aim and pulled the trigger.

Ian pumped the air rifle five times and stepped three feet and fired. The BB hit the ground. He pumped it once more and ran up to a tree.

He saw Damian's legs protruding from a bush as he lay on his stomach. He took the shot and made contact with his ankle.

"I give up Ian!" he shouted as he sat up and rubbed his wound.

Matt Jax was doped up from morphine as he lay in his hospital bed wondering what Dominique was doing. He began to think about his wife's angry words and not knowing what he should do or say to her, but to wait it out and let her cool down. "I should of just kept my big mouth shut!" he mumbled to himself.

"What was that?" Adam asked with a smile as he and Rainy stepped into his space and approached his bedside.

"Oh, hey guys." He cast his vision beyond his niece to see if anyone else came into the room.

"How are you feeling?" Rainy asked as she set a plant onto his nightstand, then cast a glance at the white gauze that was wrapped about his shoulder.

"As good as I can be, I suppose."

There was a moment of silence.

"I think I'm done bounty hunting," Matt disclosed. "It's not for me."

"Are you gonna sell the business or shut it down?"

"I won't shut it down. You, Travis, and William still need jobs."

"And maybe Nathan. He's back."

"Yea. William mentioned that when he was here." He yawned. "So how's Dominique doing?"

Rainy turned her head slightly towards Adam and sent him a visual warning.

"She packed all your shit and had us put it in the garage," Adam reported, ignoring his wife's glare.

"Ouch!" Matt responded.

THE END!

A FINAL CATCH

Keep your eye out for THE BOUNTY HUNTERS RETURN, starring William Hoffman, Dominique Kerr and her band of sons, as well as three new exciting characters to take you on a dangerous, but thrilling ride!

John 3:16	For God so loved the world that He gave His only begotten son that whosoever believes in Him should not perish, but have everlasting life.
Ephesians 1:7	In Him we have redemption through His blood, the forgiveness of sins, according to the riches of His grace.
Romans 10: 9-10	If you confess with your mouth the Lord Jesus and believe in your heart that God has raised Him from the dead, you will be saved. For with the heart one believes to righteousness, and with the mouth confession is made to salvation.